LooseId®

ISBN 10: 1-59632-819-3
ISBN 13: 978-1-59632-819-8
SOMETHING MORE
Copyright © November 2008 by Amanda Young
Originally released in e-book format in March 2007

Cover Art by Croco Designs
Cover Design by April Martinez

DISCLAIMER: Many of the acts described in our BDSM/fetish titles can be dangerous. Please do not try any new sexual practice, whether it be fire, rope, or whip play, without the guidance of an experienced practitioner. Neither Loose Id nor its authors will be responsible for any loss, harm, injury or death resulting from use of the information contained in any of its titles.

Printed in the U.S.A. by
Lightning Source, Inc.
1246 Heil Quaker Blvd
La Vergne TN 37086
www.lightningsource.com

SOMETHING MORE

Amanda Young

Chapter One

Emma Taylor wiped down the last of a dozen tables and cast a roving eye around the large room. The dark, faux leather booths and small, round tables in the middle of the floor were all clean. The oak floor was swept and mopped to a glossy shine, and the trash emptied. All she had to do was turn off the lights and lock the front door on her way out, and she would officially be on vacation.

Her job as a waitress at O'Malley's Bar and Grill wasn't the dream job she'd envisioned as a child, but it brought in a stable income and kept her bills paid, so she couldn't complain. She had it better than a lot of people.

All in all, life was pretty good. She had a roof over her head, food in her stomach, and a few good friends. Who could really expect any more than that? So what if her life was as stale as day-old doughnuts, or that she had yet to experience the big O with anything other than her handy-dandy vibrator? Things could always be worse.

Flipping over chairs and placing them upside down on top of their tables as she went along, she ambled toward the employees-only room behind the bar.

She liked her job well enough. It was trying at times, but the tips were okay, and she met new and interesting people every night. So what if her personal life was missing excitement? It wasn't from lack of trying to find Mr. Right.

She'd been there, done that, and still had the jilted-bride mementos in storage to prove it. Considering her track record with men, she was better off with her fantasies and her fingers. They wouldn't hurt her, or leave her weeping in front of the entire town on her wedding day.

Whistling the last song she'd heard on the jukebox that night, an old Patsy Cline tune about heartbreak, she moseyed into the dark break room. Guided by memory alone, she went straight to the breaker box and flipped the light switches off.

In the dark, she grabbed her coat off the hook behind the door and shrugged it onto her shoulders as she wound her way around the bar and the tables standing between her and the exit.

Seven days and nights, all to herself, awaited her. She didn't know exactly what she would do during her down time, other than relax and ignore the rest of the world, but doing absolutely nothing sounded like pure heaven.

For a full week, she could lock herself in her house, read to her heart's content, and be the overall homebody she really was. No waiting tables, no forced small talk with patrons to ensure a good tip, no nothing. She could hardly wait.

* * *

In his private apartment over the bar, Will O'Malley watched Emma get into her car and drive away. Only after her taillights faded and winked out in the distance did he release the sheer curtain over his bedroom window and stumble across the room to his lover, Paul, who lay snoring quietly in bed.

Every night, he watched to make sure Emma reached her car safely. He didn't particularly care for her working the closing shift at the bar he and Paul co-owned, but it was the shift she preferred. On one of the many occasions he'd tried to talk her into switching with another waitress, she'd plainly told him to mind his own business in her cute little singsong voice and went about her merry way.

Why he let her get by with that, he wasn't entirely sure. The fact that she'd once been engaged to his little brother might have had something to do with it. On the other hand, it could be the guilt he carried around for being so damn attracted to her.

Emma was a beautiful woman. With her long, wavy blue-black hair and her large, luminous cerulean blue eyes, Emma was a knockout. Her flawless ivory skin and ripe curves didn't do anything to dissuade his wayward libido either.

There was just something about her, some indescribable quality that called out to him, like a moth to a flame. She was his equivalent of Pandora's box. He wanted her, had for years, but he couldn't have her. Touching her, claiming her for his own, would be the end of life as he knew it. But damn if he didn't want to try anyway.

The semi-boner in his loose cotton shorts bobbed, agreeing with him.

Slipping beneath the downy cover on his massive California king bed, he wrapped an arm around Paul and snuggled up to the man he loved. What would Paul think if he knew his lover was fantasizing about a woman? A woman who could have been his sister-in-law, had his dopey kid brother actually gone through with their wedding. Instead, he'd skipped town with one of Emma's so-called friends, mere minutes before the ceremony.

It was one thing to fantasize about a woman. Paul had known two years ago, when he'd come into the relationship, that Will was bisexual and had accepted that a third person might occasionally share their bed. That wasn't an issue. Lusting after a woman who was practically family and a decade younger than he was the problem.

Paul snuffled against his pillow and wriggled his butt back against Will's groin. "Mmm," he murmured, his sinfully rich, deep voice, drowsy. "It's about time you brought your sexy ass to bed."

"I'm sorry, babe. I didn't mean to wake you."

Paul reached behind him and grabbed Will's wrist. He pressed it against the swollen flesh straining against his pajama bottoms. "I was already up."

Will snickered. "So I feel." He squeezed his partner's tumescent cock, his thumb glancing off the shallow dip beneath the flared head.

Paul moaned and turned his head, brushing a quick kiss over Will's lips. "That feels good, but how about stroking me a little harder."

Will slipped his hand under the elastic waistband of Paul's pajama bottoms and tugged on them. "I can do you one better, but you'll have to get rid of these first."

stumble across the room to his lover, Paul, who lay snoring quietly in bed.

Every night, he watched to make sure Emma reached her car safely. He didn't particularly care for her working the closing shift at the bar he and Paul co-owned, but it was the shift she preferred. On one of the many occasions he'd tried to talk her into switching with another waitress, she'd plainly told him to mind his own business in her cute little singsong voice and went about her merry way.

Why he let her get by with that, he wasn't entirely sure. The fact that she'd once been engaged to his little brother might have had something to do with it. On the other hand, it could be the guilt he carried around for being so damn attracted to her.

Emma was a beautiful woman. With her long, wavy blue-black hair and her large, luminous cerulean blue eyes, Emma was a knockout. Her flawless ivory skin and ripe curves didn't do anything to dissuade his wayward libido either.

There was just something about her, some indescribable quality that called out to him, like a moth to a flame. She was his equivalent of Pandora's box. He wanted her, had for years, but he couldn't have her. Touching her, claiming her for his own, would be the end of life as he knew it. But damn if he didn't want to try anyway.

The semi-boner in his loose cotton shorts bobbed, agreeing with him.

Slipping beneath the downy cover on his massive California king bed, he wrapped an arm around Paul and snuggled up to the man he loved. What would Paul think if he knew his lover was fantasizing about a woman? A woman who could have been his sister-in-law, had his dopey kid brother actually gone through with their wedding. Instead, he'd skipped town with one of Emma's so-called friends, mere minutes before the ceremony.

It was one thing to fantasize about a woman. Paul had known two years ago, when he'd come into the relationship, that Will was bisexual and had accepted that a third person might occasionally share their bed. That wasn't an issue. Lusting after a woman who was practically family and a decade younger than he was the problem.

Paul snuffled against his pillow and wriggled his butt back against Will's groin. "Mmm," he murmured, his sinfully rich, deep voice, drowsy. "It's about time you brought your sexy ass to bed."

"I'm sorry, babe. I didn't mean to wake you."

Paul reached behind him and grabbed Will's wrist. He pressed it against the swollen flesh straining against his pajama bottoms. "I was already up."

Will snickered. "So I feel." He squeezed his partner's tumescent cock, his thumb glancing off the shallow dip beneath the flared head.

Paul moaned and turned his head, brushing a quick kiss over Will's lips. "That feels good, but how about stroking me a little harder."

Will slipped his hand under the elastic waistband of Paul's pajama bottoms and tugged on them. "I can do you one better, but you'll have to get rid of these first."

Chapter One

Emma Taylor wiped down the last of a dozen tables and cast a roving eye around the large room. The dark, faux leather booths and small, round tables in the middle of the floor were all clean. The oak floor was swept and mopped to a glossy shine, and the trash emptied. All she had to do was turn off the lights and lock the front door on her way out, and she would officially be on vacation.

Her job as a waitress at O'Malley's Bar and Grill wasn't the dream job she'd envisioned as a child, but it brought in a stable income and kept her bills paid, so she couldn't complain. She had it better than a lot of people.

All in all, life was pretty good. She had a roof over her head, food in her stomach, and a few good friends. Who could really expect any more than that? So what if her life was as stale as day-old doughnuts, or that she had yet to experience the big O with anything other than her handy-dandy vibrator? Things could always be worse.

Flipping over chairs and placing them upside down on top of their tables as she went along, she ambled toward the employees-only room behind the bar.

She liked her job well enough. It was trying at times, but the tips were okay, and she met new and interesting people every night. So what if her personal life was missing excitement? It wasn't from lack of trying to find Mr. Right.

She'd been there, done that, and still had the jilted-bride mementos in storage to prove it. Considering her track record with men, she was better off with her fantasies and her fingers. They wouldn't hurt her, or leave her weeping in front of the entire town on her wedding day.

Whistling the last song she'd heard on the jukebox that night, an old Patsy Cline tune about heartbreak, she moseyed into the dark break room. Guided by memory alone, she went straight to the breaker box and flipped the light switches off.

In the dark, she grabbed her coat off the hook behind the door and shrugged it onto her shoulders as she wound her way around the bar and the tables standing between her and the exit.

Seven days and nights, all to herself, awaited her. She didn't know exactly what she would do during her down time, other than relax and ignore the rest of the world, but doing absolutely nothing sounded like pure heaven.

For a full week, she could lock herself in her house, read to her heart's content, and be the overall homebody she really was. No waiting tables, no forced small talk with patrons to ensure a good tip, no nothing. She could hardly wait.

* * *

In his private apartment over the bar, Will O'Malley watched Emma get into her car and drive away. Only after her taillights faded and winked out in the distance did he release the sheer curtain over his bedroom window and

Paul didn't waste any time dragging them down his lean legs. He gave them a fling across the room and turned over onto his back. Long, tapered fingers brushed Will's mussed mahogany hair away from his face. "What do you have in mind?"

Will let his fingers do the talking for him. They traveled down the base of Paul's long, hard cock, following the delicate vein that ran down the underside, caressed the silky skin of his balls, and moved back to tease his miracle inch.

Paul lifted his hips, granting Will more room to maneuver between his firm thighs. Will leaned forward and slipped the flared knob into his mouth, laving the weeping tip with the edge of his tongue before pulling more into his mouth and exerting a gentle, teasing suck.

Callused fingers ran up and down Will's back, urging him on, silently begging for more. He heard the nightstand drawer open and close. When something landed beside him, he didn't need to look up to know it was lube.

Paul was impatient, as always, and didn't want any more teasing. He wanted the whole shebang, and he wanted it yesterday. Nothing new there, and for once, Will agreed. He was too hot, too horny, to savor the buildup and finesse the pleasure as he normally would. Tonight, he too was impatient.

Giving Paul's cock one last long suck, he pulled off and grabbed the lube. Will angled the tapered nozzle against Paul's rosebud and squeezed a generous amount out. Dexterous fingers worked it in, rubbing and massaging the slippery fluid in and out. One finger and then two slid into the tight, velvety channel, stretching it, preparing it for his cock.

Twisting his fingers, Will pushed them deeper, until Paul's hips reared up off the bed and began to canter into his touch.

Paul's voice was tight and clipped when he said, "Damn it, Will. Fuck me already!"

Will wanted to drag things out until his lover was begging for it, but he was at the end of his tether as well. His cock pulsed and wept against the sheets under his belly. He couldn't wait any longer.

The bed shifted. A scalding hot mouth wrapped around his knob and sucked hard. Heavy eyelids opened to see Paul lying on his stomach, smiling up at him around a mouthful of cock.

Rising up on his knees, he slathered a deluge of KY onto his eager prick. His eyes fell closed and he moaned, enjoying the pleasure he derived from the firm stroke of his own hand.

Between the cheeky grin and the wet suction, Will lost his cool and shuddered. He wanted in, now, before he spilled himself outside the tight clasp of his lover's ass.

He pulled himself free of Paul's lips and scooted back. In tune with his needs, Paul swiveled around and spread his legs.

Will took in the wanton sight of him lying there—his legs bent at the knee and raised, one fist lazily stroking his cock—and thought he might come from the display alone.

Paul pulled him closer, licking Will's lips and then ravaging his mouth with a kiss so potent, all he could do was relish the sinuous glide of tongues and try not to drown himself in the compelling taste of Paul's mouth.

Chest heaving, Will broke free and guided his cock in between the taut globes of Paul's ass, lining it up with the slick, wrinkled pucker, and he lost the ability to think. All he could do was feel as he pressed home, his full length squeezing into the tight channel, giving it no quarter, no chance to adjust as he plunged in.

Beneath him, Paul's back bowed, pushing him up. Will cried out, and the tight ring of muscle around him clenched down, sucking him in deeper. His balls drew up, hugging the base of his cock, and he knew that in a short amount of time he would come. But he wanted Paul to finish first.

Sliding his arm between their equally hard bellies, he wrapped his hand around Paul's stiff flesh and jerked him off with strong, slow pulls. His thumb swirled over the wet cap, hitting Paul's sweet spot with every pass.

Paul's arms locked around his neck and pulled him down for a kiss. Their firm lips crashed together. Tongues came out to duel and parry.

Electricity lanced down Will's spine and into his balls. He pulled on Paul's shaft harder, wanting him to come. Now.

Paul cursed and flung his head back against the pillow. His anus clenched down on Will's cock, milking the come from his body as Paul's ejaculate shot between them.

Will collapsed on top of Paul in a satiated heap of loose muscle. He kissed the side of Paul's corded neck, trying to catch his breath. "Damn, that was good."

"Mmm," Paul practically purred. "I'll say. Jesus, what got into you tonight?"

Will nuzzled the soft hair at Paul's nape, but didn't answer. He wasn't even sure what had caused him to be so forceful. He wasn't usually like that. Paul was the aggressor in their relationship.

He rolled onto his side, propped himself up on his elbow, and looked down at Paul. He watched as Paul's chest rose and fell, his breath growing deep and languorous as sleep pulled him under. Just like it always did right after an orgasm.

Sometimes, it still amazed him that he could be so drawn to one man. Before Paul, he was as straight as the proverbial arrow. Now, he had a hell of a bend. One about eight inches in length and curving up against his navel. Though it had taken him a while to come to grips with the attraction he felt toward Paul, he'd never been happier in a relationship. There was no doubt in his mind whatsoever that Paul was the man for him.

But what about a—

He cut that thought off before it could finish. Now was not the time to think of someone else. That would be as good as being unfaithful, which was the one thing he couldn't tolerate, even from himself.

Still, something nagged at the back of his mind. A little red devil sat on his shoulder and whispered in his ear, telling him something was missing. That there was more out there for him if he dared to reach for it.

Unfortunately, doing that could mean risking his treasured relationship with Paul. Will flopped onto his back and threw his arm over his eyes. He couldn't take the chance of that happening. Paul's love was too precious to endanger.

Chapter Two

Paul Argonaut sat behind his desk, fiddling with his latest computer software project, when a soft knock at the door caught his ear. He rose up from his seat in aggravation and crossed the room. Why did people always show up at the worst possible time? What ever happened to calling first?

He was so close to being able to pinpoint the flaw in the software he was designing for his latest client that he could taste it. All he needed was some peace and quiet, and he would be able to figure it out.

Grabbing the doorknob, he yanked open the front door and instantly felt contrite. Emma stood out on the porch, a chunky older model laptop clutched to her chest. Her curly black hair was slicked back into a high ponytail that made her look about sixteen. Luminous blue eyes ringed by dark shadows flashed in irritation.

The mutinous expression on her face said it all. Her computer had crashed yet again. What was this—the third, maybe fourth time this year?

"You know," he said, smiling at her and leaning back against the door, "I'm really starting to think you're crashing that box on purpose, just so you can come over here and flirt with me."

Emma rolled her eyes. "You wish, Paul. Now, are you going to help me out with this, or make me stand out here and beg? I just bought some really great e-books to read while I'm off, and I won't very well be able to do that if I can't even get this piece of crap to boot up."

Paul held open the door and scooted out of her way so she could squeeze by him. The smell of honeysuckle clouded the air around her, leaving a delicious trail of scent in her wake. He wanted to strip her down and see if she tasted as sweet as she smelled.

And wouldn't that just shock the hell out her?

She and everyone else in the small town of Casper Falls was under the impression he was gay. Not exactly a misguided assumption, because of his relationship with Will, but not an altogether correct one either. Very few had thought to look deeper or try to get to know the man they held responsible for corrupting Will—a seemingly straight man until Paul had arrived on the scene.

In his experience, small towns meant small-minded people, and this burg was no different than any other he'd ever lived in.

Paul was what he liked to think of as "try-sexual." He'd try anything once, then most likely do it again if he found that he liked it. He'd known as soon as puberty hit that he was attracted to both men and women, so there wasn't much he wasn't willing to give a shot, as long as it was consensual and safe.

He chuckled, amused at his own thoughts. Emma turned around and looked at him strangely. "What's so funny?"

He gave her his best lecherous grin. "Nothing. I was just thinking about something."

Emma smiled and shook her head at him. "I so don't want to know whatever put that dirty grin on your face."

"You never know. You might like it," he teased back.

She turned away, mumbling something under her breath, and set her laptop on his desk. He wasn't sure what exactly she'd said, but he caught the word "dreams" in there.

He laughed and slid a chair up to his desk for her before moving around to the other side and taking a seat for himself. "So, what's it doing now?"

"Man, I don't know. It keeps saying something about my virtual memory being too low, and then the screen goes black. I don't know what's wrong with the damn thing. You're the computer expert; you tell me."

"I won't really know anything for sure until I look at it." He fingered his short blond hair. "Would you mind if I keep it overnight? I'm working on something, and I won't be able to look at your machine until later this evening."

Paul's eyes lowered, his gaze riveted on the way she sucked her full bottom lip into her mouth and nibbled on it. Like the thought of him keeping it overnight made her nervous. That made him all the more curious. What was on her computer that she didn't want him to see?

"Sure," she finally replied hesitantly, her hands twisting together in her lap. "I'll just stop back by in the morning and get it, okay?"

"No problem, Emma. I should have it done by then. I'll get started on it right after I finish up the project I'm working on."

"Great," she said, rising to her feet. "I should probably go and let you get back to work. Thanks for doing this, Paul. You're saving me a ton of money, I can't really afford to spend right now."

Paul grinned. "Is Will that cheap?"

"No—"

Emma had started to speak, intent on saying that Will wasn't any cheaper than the next boss, when the screen screeched open. Will swaggered in and let the door slam shut behind him.

He looked from her to Paul and cocked a brow. "Did I just hear my name?"

"No," Emma repeated. "We weren't talking about you. Not really, anyway. I was just thanking Paul for taking a look at my laptop for me."

"Oh," Will answered, walking closer. He shrugged out of his dark blue jacket and laid it across the back of the cream-colored sofa. "Well, that's good to know." He grinned, the small dimples in his cheeks popping out to wink at her. "I would hate to think you and Paul were in here trading stories about me."

Paul came up behind her and laid a hand on her shoulder. "We wouldn't dare do that. Now would we, Emma?"

Emma laughed at the way he drawled out his words theatrically. "Nope. Wouldn't think of it."

Will's smile edged up a degree, making his eyes twinkle and the tips of his pearly white teeth show between his sensuous pink lips. Behind her, she could smell Paul's aftershave and feel the heat from his lean frame against her back. If Will took two steps closer, both men would be touching her and she swore her thighs would go up in flames.

Standing between Paul and Will—polar opposites of each other but equally attractive in their own ways—did strange and wonderful things to Emma's body. Strange because no one else had the ability to make her feel so hot and feverish from no more than a look; wonderful for pretty much the same reason. The attraction she felt for them reminded her she was a healthy twenty-five-year-old woman, instead of the sixty-year-old spinster she felt like most days.

A look passed between Will and Paul, causing the air around her to thicken, filling with testosterone and an underlying shimmer of sexual tension. Not that any of it was directed at her. She was just caught in the middle. But that didn't stop a woman from fantasizing or longing for the things she couldn't have. Among her favorite midnight musings was being the meat in a Will and Paul sandwich. Who could blame her? They were just so damn…masculine.

Paul with his six-foot surfer's body, all bronze skin and whipcord-lean muscle. And Will with his wide shoulders, heavily muscled frame, and deep chocolate eyes. How was a gal supposed to be alone with the two of them and not end up with moist panties and hard nipples? If there was a woman alive who could, she was a better person than Emma ever hoped to be. The best she could do was try to keep her face from reflecting her want, and resist the urge to rub her neglected and wanton pussy in their presence.

To her shame, she'd always been attracted to Will. Even when Mark, her then boyfriend, had taken her home to meet his parents, her eyes had been drawn time and again to his older brother. After the wedding fell through, she was surprised to discover that losing Will's friendship meant more to her than losing Mark. When he'd offered her a job at his pub after one of his waitresses quit on him, she was happy to accept. She jumped on the chance to be around him more often, though she knew working there would be uncomfortable on the occasions his brother came by. Thankfully, those times had been few and far between because Mark moved into the city not long after their split.

Will's relationship with Paul hadn't dimmed her lustful thoughts about him, either. If anything, throwing Paul into the equation sent her idling curiosity about him from hot to supernova. Something about two men, these two in particular, ignited her desires like no one else ever had.

That's why she'd bought the e-books.

Scouring the Internet for new romance novels, she'd come across a site she'd never seen before. It boasted having the largest selection of gay and ménage romance novels on the web. Curiosity made her read the blurbs. Picturing herself in the shoes of the heroines made her buy.

While she wasn't entirely sure she would get into the gay romances, she found that they struck a chord with her, almost, if not equally, as strong as the ones featuring women.

She'd bought several of each and downloaded them to her computer right before it took a nosedive.

This was her reason for not wanting Paul to keep the computer longer than he needed it. She trusted him, but people, even good, trustworthy ones, were inherently nosy. The last thing she wanted was for him to notice her new reading material. Paul was a tease and a bit of a flirt on his best days. There was no way he would let her live down an interest in reading about gay men and three-ways if he ever found out about it.

Just thinking about it made her cringe. She would rather have her eyelashes pulled out one by one than suffer through that hell.

Still, the man was busy and clearly doing her a favor by agreeing to look at it all. It would have been rude to demand he fix it while she waited, like he had the last several times she'd brought it by. Since she didn't have the money to take it to a professional tech, she was stuck asking for his help. She just hoped he resisted the urge to snoop through her files.

Will stepped in closer and leaned over her shoulder. He kissed Paul, and she was afraid she would hyperventilate. His arm inadvertently brushed the side of her breast, and Emma thought she would melt into a puddle of goo.

She was going to hell. That's what was sure to happen, when she committed two of the seven deadly sins every time she was around them. She lusted after their bodies and envied their love for each other.

She had to get out of there. Now. Before she did or said something she couldn't take back.

Emma jolted back, her head slamming into Paul's hard chest, and ducked away from them. "Sorry," she mumbled over her shoulder as she hurried to the door. "I have to go. I just remembered something important I forgot to do."

Without waiting for a reply, she closed the door behind her and ran.

"What was that all about?" Will said, leaning back against the desk, with his thick forearms crossing his broad chest. "You'd think she hadn't ever seen us kiss before."

"Yeah, but I don't think she's ever been within touching distance of us at the time, meathead." Paul scratched his head, his smile broadening. "I think our little Emma has a crush on you."

Will felt the smile slide off his face. "Whatever." He stood up and walked into the kitchen, with Paul hot on his heels.

He didn't even want to joke about that. The thought of Emma possibly returning the feelings he had for her scared the hell out of him. He wanted to have his cake and eat it too; he wanted to keep Paul, but he sure as hell wanted Emma. He wasn't entirely sure he could turn her down if the opportunity presented itself.

"What do you mean, whatever? Haven't you ever noticed the way Emma gets all quiet and starts blushing whenever you're around her? I think it's cute."

Will pulled open the fridge and grabbed an ice-cold longneck off the shelf. He swallowed half of it before studying Paul. The slight tilt to his lips and the gleam of heat in his eyes told Will that Paul was up to something.

He swallowed down the last half of his beer and pitched the empty into the garbage pail from across the room. "Forget it."

"Forget what?"

"Whatever it is you've got up your sleeve."

"Who, me?"

Will snickered. "Can the innocent act, buddy. It doesn't work anymore."

Paul strode across the linoleum and wrapped his arms around Will. A couple of inches shorter than Paul's six foot two, Will had to look up to meet Paul's heavily fringed jade-green eyes. One arm around Will's shoulders, Paul's other hand traced the contours of Will's side before swooping lower to cup his groin. Paul cocked an inquisitive eyebrow at him when he felt the monster wood Will was sporting in his Dockers. His cock had been hard as a spike ever since he'd had the pleasure of Paul's firm lips against his, and Emma's soft curves rubbing up against him at the same time. Shit. It wasn't like he could help it; the bastard had a mind of its own. They didn't call it a head for nothing.

Paul's hand stroked the ridge of Will's erection through his pants. "I'm not the one playing innocent here. For somebody who's mighty opposed to even considering bringing Emma in as a third, you've got a hell of a hard-on."

His hand trailed down to knead Will's drawn-up sac. Will tried to keep his mind on what they were talking about, but it was damn hard to do while his balls were trying to crawl up into his body. "We...agreed that...we wouldn't ...bring in anyone we knew. It's safer that way. No misunderstandings."

Fingers tugged at his pants. Cool air washed over his feverish cock. Paul dropped to his knees and replaced the cool air with the sweltering heat of his mouth. Tongue, teeth, and palate all worked together to drive Will out of his mind. He would have agreed to anything, as long as Paul didn't stop the hard, wet pulls up and down his cock.

With one hand on the counter to keep himself upright, Will buried the other in Paul's hair and started to fuck Paul's mouth the way he wanted. "Oh, yeah. Oh, fuck. Just like that, baby."

Long, fast plunges in and out of Paul's mouth brought Will to the brink and tossed him over the edge of the precipice. His orgasm started in his lower back and exploded up through his balls to the end of his cock, filling Paul's mouth with his seed.

Paul let him free with a wet plop, but continued to lick Will's softening penis until nothing was left of his climax. Seemingly satisfied that he'd gotten it all, he tucked Will back into his pants and eased the zipper back up.

"See, that proves it," Paul said, rising to his feet.

"Proves what?" Will asked, his mind still clouded by his orgasm. He was too relaxed, too sated, to understand what Paul was talking about.

"You like the idea of getting Emma between us."

Will's forehead wrinkled. He could feel a headache coming on. "How does you sucking me off prove that I want to fuck Emma?"

"You never, *never*, get off that easy or that fast."

Will scowled. "So? Maybe you just look extra hot today."

"Don't give me that bullshit, Will. You're so hot for her, steam almost came out of your ears when I brought it up. The only thing that could have made you shoot faster would've been Emma on her knees helping me blow you."

Will sighed. He figured he might as well fess up. He'd never hear the end of it now anyway. He leaned against Paul, resting his head on his lover's shoulder. "So what?" Will whispered. "What if I do want her? It doesn't matter. I'm not going to do anything about it."

Paul combed his hands through Will's hair, soothing him. "Why not? If she's willing—and I'm betting she would be—what difference would it make? It's not like we haven't shared women before."

"It's not the same with Emma. I want more than one night with her."

Paul stiffened, and Will wished he could take the words back. "What are you saying?"

Will drew in a ragged breath. "I love you. You know that. But there's always been this...connection between her and me. I see Emma, and I want her. I can't make it go away. Even when she was with Mark, God help me, I wanted her." He'd already said enough, but he might as well get the rest off his chest while he was at it. "I want you both."

Paul guffawed, his burst of laughter rumbling loud in Will's ear against him.

Will pulled back and stared up at his lover. "What is so funny? I just told you my darkest secret, and you're laughing."

"You want us both—that's all? That's what you were so worried about? Jesus, you really had me going there for a minute."

Will harrumphed and walked out of the room. Sometimes there was just no talking to Paul.

Chapter Three

On her way home, Emma swung by the diner and picked up the to go order she'd called in before dropping her computer off with Paul. The entire time, her mind replayed the sight of Paul and Will kissing, her squashed in between them. She overanalyzed every nuance of that moment—the hot looks that passed between the men, the different smells of their cologne, the heat radiating from their muscled bodies pressing against her—but most of all the tension surrounding them and the sharp influx of desire she'd felt.

When she pulled into her driveway a few minutes later, she could honestly say she didn't remember a single thing she'd said to anyone or vice versa. If not for the plastic bag and delicious smell of thick, meaty marinara sauce emanating from within, she would've sworn she'd driven straight home.

Shaking her head at her foolish and dreamful musings, she grabbed her dinner and headed into the house, planning to drop off the dinner she'd picked up for her mom before heading over to the apartment she kept above the garage.

"Mom, I'm here. Where are you?" Emma yelled as she walked in the open front door.

"I'm in here, dear."

Emma followed her mom's voice into the kitchen and found her sitting at the table, a deck of cards spread out before her in a game of solitaire.

Her mom was a beautiful woman. Only in her early forties, Suzanne was still young enough to pass as Emma's older sister instead of her parent. A fact that irked Emma to death when she was young, but one she grew to appreciate as she herself aged.

Her mom's rich chestnut hair and smooth, unlined complexion did not give the impression of a woman in her early forties. Emma hoped she aged half as gracefully as her mom had. Lord knew she hadn't inherited anything else from her. They were as opposite as day and night in both personality and appearance.

Her mom was tall, tan, slender, and had a sleek mane of smooth, straight hair that she highlighted every spring and darkened every fall. Emma, on the other hand, was short, curvy, pale as ivory, and had hair that would make a saint curse if they had to deal with her untamable frizzy curls.

Emma figured she must have inherited her looks from her father's side. She could only assume, because she had no idea who he was. Pregnant at seventeen, her mom refused to name the father of her unborn child, and she'd stuck to it. Even Emma's incessant badgering over the years had produced not a single hint of who had sired her.

She sat the bag down on the table. "I brought dinner."

Her mom glanced up, smiled at her, and then returned her gaze to her card game. "Oh, well, thank you, dear. Just put my salad in the fridge for me, would you? I'll eat later."

Emma smiled, amused by her mom's antics. The woman had a one-track mind. A good thing, except when she centered it on her only child and went into full lecture mode. That was a torture best escaped if at all possible.

These days, the woman was a complete nag when it came to the subject of Emma finding a man and settling down. Why she felt that way, when she herself had never been married or even in any long-term relationship, was beyond guessing.

Emma stuffed the garden salad in the fridge next to the Slim-Fast and coffee creamer and grabbed her big styrofoam container of ziti. "I'm leaving, Mom. Holler at me if you need anything, okay?"

"Sure, dear, you go on ahead," Emma's mother muttered absently.

Emma made it to the front door and had her hand on the knob, ready to turn it, when she heard five dreaded little words come out of Suzanne's mouth.

"Emma, do you have plans tonight?"

Groaning, she turned around and faced her mom. "Yes, I do. I plan to stay in, eat my dinner, and order a movie."

Here it comes. In three...two...one...

"Those aren't the kind of plans I meant, young lady, and you know it. You're on vacation, for goodness' sake. Why don't you go out and enjoy it like the other girls your age, instead of cloistering yourself up in that tiny apartment above the garage?" She patted perfectly manicured fingers over her flawlessly coiffed hair. "You're never going to find a man if you don't go out and look for him. You think Mark is sitting around, pining after you somewhere?"

Emma bit her lip until the anger over that last remark passed, and then she calmly and quietly spoke. "No, I'm sure he isn't. I'm sure he's out banging the flavor of the moment." She sighed, utterly sick of having the same discussion. "I am not pining after Mark, Mom. It's been four years; I think I'm over it by now. I do not harbor any hidden designs of ever getting back together with Mark O'Malley."

I want his older brother instead, she thought, and then immediately felt bad for it. Will couldn't ever be hers, but damn if she didn't want him anyway. *Maybe that's why I want him?* Perhaps it was the safety in knowing that she'd never win his affection. She could admire him from afar and never have to worry about holding on to his attention and failing like she had with Mark.

"All the same, honey, you're not getting any younger. It's much easier to land a man when you're young than when you get older. By then, all the good ones will be taken."

Emma sighed and tried not to raise her voice. "I don't need a man to make me happy. I'm perfectly fine with my life the way it is."

"I know you *think* you are, dear. But that's only because you don't know what you're missing. And what about grandkids? I would like to have some grandbabies before I'm too old to play with them."

"Give me a break, will you? You're barely past forty. I think there's plenty of time left for you to enjoy any kids I ever have, *if* I ever decide to have any."

Her mom opened her mouth. "I—"

"Mom," Emma interrupted, "I'm going to the apartment. My food is getting cold. We can argue about this later, all right?"

Not waiting for her mom to reply, she opened the door and walked through it. How many times could they argue about her needing a husband, anyway?

* * *

This was beyond perfect.

Paul stared at small screen of Emma's laptop and snickered like a kid who'd just found his father's stash of dirty magazines. He knew she read romances. He'd seen those before. But her latest purchases went a bit farther than that. The newest titles in her digital library focused on relationships between gay men, or two bisexual men who shared a woman.

He opened his mouth to yell for Will, who was lying in bed watching a movie, but thought better of it at the last second. Why throw gas on the huge bonfire of responsibility the man carried around on those wide shoulders of his for nothing? There was still every chance that his plan to get the three of them together could blow up in his face.

A devious smile on his face and a tent in the front of his loose grey sweatpants, Paul propped his hands behind his head and relaxed back in his reclining desk chair. Will wasn't the only one craving a taste of Emma's sweetness.

Paul missed a woman's gentle touch. The few one-night stands he and Will had here and there were fun; he wouldn't lie and say otherwise. But he wanted something more…something permanent. Knowing Will felt the same way, even if he hadn't put it in those exact words, freed Paul from his worries about hurting Will by bringing the subject up, and opened up a whole world of possibilities.

Now, he had to convince the woman they'd both had their eye on to give them a chance to prove their love and devotion. He would bet good money that getting Emma to agree wouldn't be nearly as hard as persuading Will.

* * *

Long after Paul began to snore softly beside him, Will lay awake in bed, his thoughts in turmoil over his mixed emotions and the way Paul had reacted to his earlier confession. All through dinner and later as the quiet set in, he'd wanted to broach the subject again, but hadn't.

Will was almost afraid to hear what Paul would say. He knew his lover well and didn't want to hear about any half-baked plans he had in the works that would ruin the balance they'd found with each other.

Paul was a firm believer in making dreams come true whenever possible. Will could practically see the wheels spinning in Paul's head when he'd admitted his attraction to Emma. What kind of crazy idea would Paul come up with to curb the desire he felt?

Will foresaw a long night, he and Paul trolling the clubs looking for an Emma look-alike, and cringed. He was tired of the game. Tired of the one-night stands they seldom even had anymore with nameless, faceless women that meant less than nothing to him.

He wanted more than that. Will wanted to settle down, to have a family of his own. Paul didn't quite fit into that equation, but he loved him too much to let him go. He wanted a wife and kids, but he needed Paul. Paul was his best friend, the other half of his soul. Without him, Will wouldn't want to get up every morning and face the world.

Will punched his pillow. He pressed his face into it and sighed. There was no way to win. He couldn't have everything he wanted.

He fell into a restless sleep. Visions of both Emma and Paul hurt because of his desires tormented him into the early hours of morning.

Chapter Four

His chest bare, black jogging shorts riding low on his lean hips, Will staggered into the apartment after his morning run. Leaving the door open behind him, he headed through the living room and into the kitchen, where a cold bottle of water awaited his parched throat.

Clean sweat glistened across his broad shoulders and matted the sparse, dark hair sprinkled between his taut pecs and arrowed down beneath the waistband of his shorts. Around his forehead and temples, damp, curling tendrils of thick hair clung to his face.

It was a great morning to be outside. The temperature was just right; not too hot, not too cold. He hadn't been able to resist getting outside and pounding away some of his tension on the sidewalk. Five miles later, he felt like a new man. Albeit a tired and exhausted one.

Leftover surges of adrenaline pumped through his veins as he lifted a bottle of water out of the fridge and drained it. The condensation on the plastic slid over his hand and dripped down onto his throat.

"Have a nice jog?" Will turned away from the fridge as Paul entered the room. He gladly accepted the white hand towel Paul held out to him.

"Oh, yeah, a great one," Will replied, blotting down his face and neck while Paul watched. Will returned the favor, sneaking a good look at his lover around each swipe of the towel over his damp face.

Paul wore a pair of snug, dark blue jeans and nothing more. The jeans themselves were zipped but unbuttoned, hanging precariously off Paul's narrow hips. The pair was a favorite of Will's. They clung to Paul's long, powerfully built legs and cupped his tight ass. Like Will's hand wanted to do. Every time he wore them, Will wanted to rip them off and get to the good stuff underneath.

The bright morning sun shone in through the windows, highlighting Paul's smooth bronze skin over chiseled abs, lickable stiff copper nipples, and well-defined shoulders, cut with lean corded muscles. Will's cock thickened and lifted, straining to be free of its cloth barrier. Saliva pooled in his mouth as he mentally willed the zipper on Paul's jeans to lower and bare all.

Neither man enjoyed wearing more clothes than they had to when at home. Being just the two of them, they often closed the blinds and happily sauntered around the house in the buff. Something Will was eternally grateful for at the moment because his penis was engorged to the point of breaking off. Both the cause and cure stood right in front of him.

"Come here," Will urged Paul with a come-hither twist of his fingers.

Paul's eyes fell to the prominent bulge in Will's crotch. He ran the tip of his pink tongue over his bottom lip, leaving behind a trail of moisture. Will felt what little blood remained above his waistline drain into his cock. Paul looked up, meeting Will's eyes, and gave a little shake of his head. "Nope. Don't think I can do that."

Grinning like a fool, Paul backed up and stepped over the brass strip that separated the cream ceramic tile in the kitchen from the hardwood floor in living room. "You have to catch me."

A predatory smile on his face, Will advanced toward him.

* * *

After a long and boring night, Emma fell asleep late and didn't awake until close to noon the following day.

Jumping out of the bed, she scrambled to pull herself together. She yanked a brush through her hair, secured it back in a lopsided ponytail and threw on an old, threadbare pair of jeans and a T-shirt. Her unhindered breasts felt so nice, she decided to forego the bra for a change. Something she wouldn't normally dare to do if she were going out in public.

Today though, she had no such plans. She intended to drive the short distance over to Will and Paul's, pick up her laptop, then return straight home. Emma was anxious to kick back and read some of the steamy books she'd bought. After the torrid dream she'd had the night before—being the cheese in a Paul and Will sandwich—this afternoon would be a great time to try out one of the new mail order toys she'd bought recently. That, however, would have to wait until she got back.

Living just a few miles away from her destination, the drive over was quick. She jogged up the back stairs leading to their apartment and raised her hand to knock. What she saw through the screen door caused her knuckles to pause in midair and fall uselessly back to her side. Mouth as dry as the Sahara, Emma's gaze zoomed in on what was happening inside.

She started to slam her eyelids closed, only to change her mind. Yes, she wanted to blink and make sure what she saw was real, but there was no way she would miss out on a moment of this, just in case her eyesight was to be believed. She wanted to turn around and allow them privacy. No, that was a lie. Emma wanted to stay and watch, but she didn't want to get caught doing it.

Paul groaned, the sound of his passionate cry reaching out to her, wrapping around her like a hot, mind-smothering blanket, and her choice was made. There was no way she was moving. This glimpse of them together would fuel her fantasies for years to come and probably up the stock value of Duracell batteries.

Paul was bent over his desk, his chest pressed into its gleaming cherry finish. Corded muscles stood out in his neck and shoulders. Indigo jeans puddled around his ankles. From where she stood, she saw his fist stroking the long, pale jut of his hard cock.

Sodomizing him from behind, Will wore his birthday suit and not a stitch else. Plastered against Paul's lower half, Will's taut ass cheeks flexed and hollowed with each forward lunge. One wide hand spanned Paul's hip, holding him close. Eyes closed, Will's head tilted slightly back and away from

Emma, allowing her to study both men as they took their pleasure from each another.

Her mesmerized gaze locked on their connected groins and froze there, watching. Will shuttled his cock in and out of Paul's ass with long, deep thrusts. Every time he pulled back, she caught a brief glimpse of his glistening shaft. Then he would rotate his hips and plunged back inside, grinding his groin against Paul's taut buttocks.

Paul shifted, cursing, and arched up higher on his toes, shoving back into Will for more. Leanly contoured muscles rippled, flexing as his back bowed and his forehead lowered to the desk.

He cried out, "Shit! Fuck me harder, Will," and Emma thought she'd wet herself, so much moisture rushed to fill her panties. Her cunt throbbed, clenching emptily. Emptiness she desperately wanted filled by one of—both of—the men before her. She tried to shove those fantasies down, back into the locked chest where all her forbidden desires dwelled. They wouldn't have it. Her needs fought and resisted, demanding attention.

"You like that, don't you?" Will replied, leaning down over Paul, his fingers digging into Paul's hips. His thrusts began to pick up speed, furiously pumping his cock into Paul's ass, over and over. "You can't get enough of my hard dick reaming your tight little ass, can you?"

"Never enough, Will. Feels so good, baby. More…give me more."

Will groaned. He pressed a lingering kiss to the back of Paul's nape. "Mmm, Paul, I can't…I'm gonna…"

"Let go. Come for me, baby. I'm so close…right there."

Paul shouted, crying out his release. His muscles visibly tensed. Ropy jets of opaque semen splashed against the wooden desk, dripping down its side.

Will uttered something incoherent, thrust hard one last time, and held himself deep. His hips worked in little shaky circles as his climax barreled over him.

Seeing both men come, Emma felt an answering throb seep inside her channel. One touch, one breath, and she would have been right there with them. The single grain of common sense she held onto was the only thing that kept her from slipping her hand inside her jeans and finishing herself off.

Will's hand smoothed over Paul's flank, rubbing and caressing in an odd little figure eight pattern. Emma imagined that gentle touch did as much to soothe him as it did Paul. The sweet gesture also served to remind her that she was on the outside looking in. A Peeping Tom, rather than an active participant in their lovemaking.

Cheeks burning with embarrassment, she cast one last covetous glance inside. And saw Paul's flushed face turn in her direction.

He was staring right at her.

Emma gasped, taking a step back. Paul winked, an amused tilt to his kiss-swollen lips. She swiveled around and flew down the stairs, her feet thumping loudly on the wooden steps as she hurried away.

The entire drive home she prayed for the asphalt road to open up and swallow her car. With her in it.

How was she ever going to be able to face them again?

* * *

Paul wiped the smile off his face before Will could see it. The man was blissfully unaware that they had had an audience during their lovemaking. It was shame she hadn't shown up a few minutes sooner or she would have seen a lot more than she did. Will was the self-proclaimed king of rimming, and who was Paul to stop him from doing something he liked so well?

That thought almost forced another grin.

Emma was no doubt mortified that he'd caught her watching them. Like he hadn't hoped things would work out that way. Otherwise, he wouldn't have been lax enough to leave the door open when he knew Will was going to fuck him right in front of it. He may be kinky, but he wasn't into advertising their sex life to all of God and country.

Will pulled back, his softening member sliding out with a wet squelch. He leaned forward and pressed his lips softly against Paul's. "Thank you, baby. That was just what I needed."

Paul smirked. "Don't thank me. You did all the work."

Will scooted back, and grabbed the discarded hand towel at his feet. He used it to clean Paul and then himself of their spent passion before pulling up his shorts.

Paul pulled himself up off the desk and yanked up his own pants. He winced a little as the rough denim scraped over the sensitive flange of his cock. "So," he said, while zipping up. "What do you have planned for the rest of the day?"

Will shuffled into the kitchen and brought them each out a bottle of Evian. He pitched Paul's over to him. "I need to go down to the bar and do some paperwork. Also, there's a shipment of liquor coming in that I want to be there for. I think they've been shorting us a bottle of Beam." He took a long swallow of water. "What about you?"

"I finished up that software Biotech wanted, so I'll probably run that over to them. On my way back, I thought I would drop off Emma's laptop."

Will nodded, his face going thoughtful. "Say hi for me. I'm going to go get a quick shower."

Paul watched Will walk down the hall before throwing on the polo shirt he'd discarded across the back of the couch earlier. He grabbed his briefcase, Emma's laptop, and out the door he went.

Chapter Five

After dropping his software off at Biotech, Paul drove straight to Emma's. He pulled up outside the small, white clapboard house Emma's mother owned, and killed the engine.

There he continued to sit for several long moments, feeling a heavy burden of doubt on his shoulders. Although he was relieved to be finished with one project, another bigger task faced him. One much more important than the asinine, user-friendly software he'd just completed.

It was a good thing he wasn't going to be busy, because he feared he was about to have his hands full. It was one thing to arrange a temporary fling. Orchestrating a happily-ever-after deal was something else altogether. Something he'd never undertaken before. He would be flying by the seat of his pants every step of the way.

Paul slid out of his Beamer and slammed the door. His car blocked in Emma's, but there were no other vehicles in the driveway. Apparently her mother was still at the hospital. He remembered Emma once saying that, as a registered nurse, she worked rotating shifts in the emergency room at County West.

He ignored the front door and walked around back to the private entrance to Emma's small apartment. Though she didn't technically live at home, Paul wondered how she could stand living within shouting distance of her mother. Then again, if her parent was anything like the spoiled snob that sent him off to boarding school at ten years old, he figured she wouldn't have been there. Coming from the world's most dysfunctional family, the dynamics of other families always fascinated him.

At the top of the narrow stairway, he rang the bell. When that garnered no response, he figured she was either hoping he would go away or that the damn thing didn't work. Either way, she was home and he wasn't leaving until he saw her.

Paul knocked, waited a breath, and then knocked again. "Emma. I know you're home." No response. "I've got your laptop. Don't you want it back?"

The deadbolt clicked back, and the door swung inward an inch. The side of Emma's face popped into view. "Go away."

She tried to slam the door shut, but Paul's foot intercepted her by squeezing into the opening. "Open the door, Emma. I just want to talk."

The one eye Paul could see narrowed. "About what?"

"Do you really want to have this conversation through the door? I'm sure your neighbors would *love* to hear what I have to say."

Paul chuckled when the door closed and he heard the chain sliding back. He knew that would do the trick. She was much too concerned about what people thought of her.

Emma opened the door and stepped back, allowing him to pass. Paul glanced around the large open room that made up her entire living quarters.

Everything was decorated in shades of mauve and blue. A small, light blue loveseat and chair divided the sitting area from the bedroom area. On the other side of the room, a double four-poster bed sat against the wall, a velvet comforter spread over the mattress, mauve throw pillows scattered over the top. Separated by a door that he imagined led into the bathroom was a small nook containing a mini-fridge and a tiny glass dining table.

"Nice place," Paul murmured, as Emma shut the door. He turned back and held out her laptop. "It's fixed. All ready to rock."

She accepted it and sidestepped around him. "Thanks." Emma sat down in the chair, folding her legs underneath her. She motioned toward the loveseat.

Paul sat across from her. He propped one ankle over the opposite knee, folded his hands over it, and waited for her to say something. He figured by the way she fidgeted in her seat and chewed on her bottom lip, he wouldn't have to wait long. He wasn't disappointed.

"Look. I'm sorry about earlier today. I didn't mean to see what I did. But you guys left the door open and—"

"It's okay, Emma," Paul interrupted. "I knew you were coming by. The door was left open on purpose. I wanted you to watch."

Emma's blue eyes grew round as the sun. "What?" she sputtered. "Why?" A line formed between her brows, and her look changed from horrified to furious. "Oh, wait. I get it. You and Will thought you would give the lonely spinster a thrill, huh?"

"Now wait a minute, Emma. I never—"

She shook her head and held up a hand, shushing him. "I can just hear the two of you now. 'Poor Emma hasn't gotten laid since Mark dumped her. Why don't we just show her what she's missing? Maybe then she'll get back up on the saddle and start dating again.' Is that what this is about, Paul?"

By the time she had finished, her hands were waving in the air and Paul was slightly afraid she was going to have an apoplexy. He'd forgotten how overemotional women could be sometimes. It was actually kind of cute. Of course, he wasn't stupid enough to tell her that. Dealing with a female was going to be a refreshing change from what he was used to.

"Wait," he said, just catching onto something she'd said. "You haven't been laid since you and Mark split?"

Her eyes spit fire at him.

"I'm sorry," he quickly backpedaled. "It wasn't anything like that. I promise, Emma. Hell, Will didn't even know you were there so you can't bring his name into it." Paul leaned forward. "I guess I screwed this up. I just thought that if you were all hyped up from seeing us together, it would be easier to talk you into doing what I wanted. I didn't expect you to get pissed off about it."

Emma's eyes narrowed into squinty aqua slits. "Talk me into what, Paul?"

Damn. She was a smart cookie. He was hoping she wouldn't have caught his slip of the tongue. "Well...I know you have a thing for Will—"

"I do not have a thing for Will," she interjected.

"Yeah, right. That's why you're always staring at him when you think no one's looking and why you take off like a scared rabbit if he comes near you."

Emma scowled. "I do not."

"Whatever, Emma. That's not the point anyway. You see, things are good between me and Will—damn good—but we both want something more. Something I think you could give us if you're willing. I know for a fact that Will's in love with you. Hell, I'm halfway there myself. And I think the three of us would be great together if you just gave us a shot."

* * *

Emma sat with her mouth agape long after Paul left. The things he said swirled in her head, taunting her, teasing her with the promise of what could be.

After dropping the proverbial bomb into her lap, Paul urged her to give what he'd said some thought and get back to him. He had also made her promise not to say anything to Will, admitting he'd told Will nothing of the proposition he'd just made.

That in itself made her curious. If he was so sure Will had feelings for her, then why hadn't he been in on the suggestion? Had Paul made it all up, like some great April Fool's joke?

Emma scrubbed her hands over her face. Paul may be a tease but he wasn't cruel. He wouldn't intentionally hurt a fly, much less her. He'd meant what he said.

Her cell phone rang from across the room, and she got up to answer it. Picking up the tiny flip phone, she looked at the caller ID. *Mom*. She rolled her eyes. A lecture was the last thing she needed at the moment. "Yes, Mom."

"And hello to you too, dear. Listen, I was talking to some of the girls here at work and Wanda, a nice resident on my shift, was telling me all about her single brother and—"

"No, Mom. I'm not going out with your friend's brother. No blind dates! How many times do I have to tell you that? If I want a man, I'll go out and find my own. I do *not* need you to pick one out for me."

"But—"

"No buts, Mom. I love you, but keep your nose out of my love life. It's none of your business."

"You know I'm only looking out for your best interest, dear. I just want you to be happy. That's what all parents want for their children."

Emma sighed into the phone. Her mom was the queen of the subtle guilt trip. Now she felt like a heel for snapping at her. "I'm sorry, Mom. I didn't mean to be snarky, but I'm perfectly happy with things the way they are. Now, I really have to get off the phone. I was..." *Damn. Where was a good excuse when you need it?* "I was just about to get into the tub. I'll talk to you later. I love you, bye."

Emma hung up fast, before her mom could utter another word. No sense in giving her an opening when the woman was so good at finding them on her own.

And just so her excuse for getting off the phone wouldn't be a complete lie, Emma started stripping off her clothes on her way to the bathroom. Maybe a nice, long, hot bath would help her clear her head.

Chapter Six

Will and Paul sat in the bar, surrounded by a rowdy crowd of regular bar patrons and acquaintances alike, slugging back one cold beer after another.

Hours earlier, Paul had come clean about his talk with Emma. That, and the fact they hadn't heard back from her one way or the other, had prompted a late night bender.

They could have consumed any one of the myriad bottles of liquor they kept in reserve at the apartment, but neither man wanted to stay in.

The upside to living above the bar was neither had to worry about being the designated driver. They could both get rip-roaring drunk if they wanted, and only have to crawl back up the stairs to get home afterward.

Three pitchers into the night, and Paul was smashed. Will had a buzz, but not much more.

Will wasn't sure what to think about Paul's admission. On the one hand, if Emma took him up on his hasty proposal, Will would be eternally grateful. On the other, if Emma turned them down and wouldn't have anything to do with either of them afterward, Will was going to kick his lover's cute little ass.

Being near her without the right to touch her, claim her for his very own the way he wanted, was torture at times, but it was better than nothing. Will was desperate enough that he would take Emma however he could get her. Even if it did mean a lot of nights beating off in the shower before crawling into bed with Paul.

He supposed he could have let Paul take care of the frantic itch Emma caused, but it didn't seem right to do that. To make love to one, while thinking of the other was just plain wrong in his book. So, he suffered it out. It wouldn't be the first time he'd been forced to take matters into his own hands, and he didn't figure it would be the last. Sometimes a man just had to do what he had to do. It was a fact of life.

Paul's voice bellowed into his ear over the loud staccato beat of the twangy country song currently blaring out of the jukebox in the corner. "How 'bout 'nother pitcher?"

The soft slur to his words told Will that Paul had already drank more than enough for both of them. Will glanced over at the waitress Bearing down on them and mouthed the word "nonalcoholic." It was easier than arguing about whether or not they were going to buy any more booze tonight.

Buxom, red-haired Tina—the only waitress who'd been working at the bar since before his dad had passed it on to Will a decade before—winked at him to signal she'd read his lips loud and clear before hustling back around the bar to fetch their order.

Paul slumped over on Will's shoulder, his weight heavy but welcome. One of his hands wandered down the front of Will's shirt and toyed with the three unused buttons on his navy polo. "I'm sorry, Bear," Paul slurred, using the nickname he only used when he thought he was in trouble. "I really thought she'd go for it. Didn't 'spect her to turn me down."

Will kissed the ruffled fringe of wheat blond hair falling down over Paul's forehead. He didn't dare do more, not in public. His regular bar patrons knew they were a couple; most of them accepted it, but that didn't mean they would be comfortable with a show. "Emma hasn't turned us down, yet. She just hasn't said anything. Now don't worry about it anymore. Either way, you meant well."

Long agile fingers rubbed over Will's crotch under the table, coaxing his cock to lengthen and fill. Paul gently squeezed, his thumb running over the flared ridge at the tip. "Love you, Bear. Jus' want you happy."

Will placed his hand over Paul's, stopping the tease before he went too far. "Love you too, baby."

He pushed Paul up as Tina drew near with their fresh pitcher. She set the frosted carafe in the middle of the table, sloshing a bit over the rim and onto the laminated wood surface. "Here you go, boss."

"Thanks, Tina," Will replied, smiling his thanks as she hurried off to wait on her other tables.

While Paul was busy clumsily pouring himself fake beer and guzzling it down, Will glanced around the bar and took in the scene. To his right, a group of older regulars sat at the bar. The younger crowd milled around, hitting on anything with a pulse. The way they avoided one another, like there was an invisible wall between the young twenty-somethings and the forty-plus age bracket, gave Will a whole passel of things to ruminate on. Like how old he was.

At thirty-one, Paul was four years younger than him. That didn't seem like such a huge age gap. And yet thinking about Emma, who was all of twenty-five, made him feel like a dirty old lecher.

Shit. Who was he kidding? There were too many bridges to build over, too many issues that stood in the way of a relationship between the three of them, for it to ever have a snowball's chance in hell of working.

Paul belched, loud and abrasively. Then he laughed like it was the funniest thing he'd ever done. Will rolled his eyes, and tried not to sigh like an old man, while watching his lover's antics.

He had to tell Paul to call the whole thing off. And he would, first thing in the morning, when Paul was sober and able to carry on an adult conversation.

*　*　*

Emma laid her head back against the pink bath pillow behind her head. Steam rose from the hot, honeysuckle-scented water and loosened her taut muscles. Other than that, the water's sensual glide against her skin was not having the effect she'd hoped. If anything, it ramped up her desire, causing her thoughts to center around Paul's offer and what it would be like to take him up on it.

Letting her eyes fall closed, Emma pictured Will and Paul as she'd seen them earlier—their bodies moving, rigid muscles flexing as they made love. What would it be like to be in the middle of the love they so clearly felt for each other? Would she feel it as much, or more, than the lust she harbored for their bodies?

Their images shifted behind her lids until she saw herself appear between them. She was in Paul's place, bent over the desk. Will's fingers glided down her side, soothing her, stroking her, and her own slim fingers tried to mimic what she experienced in her imagination. Slick with water, they glided down the side of her ribs, into the valley of her waist, and over the curve of her hip. Goosebumps that had nothing to do with the temperature popped out over the surface of her skin. Everywhere she touched tingled, like lightning in a bottle.

The picture behind her eyes expanded, pushing her dream lovers into motion. Paul moved before her, sitting upon the desk, and offered his cock up to her mouth. He ran the fat bulb over her lips, tempting, teasing her to flick her tongue out and taste him.

Will shifted behind her, the hard press of his penis gliding wetly through the lips of her sex, tunneling up and through the cheeks of her bottom. The hot, flared ridge of his head caught on her clit, bumping it, nudging her need higher.

Concentration torn, she didn't know who to give her full attention to. She wanted it all. To taste Paul, and to feel Will buried deep inside of her.

Will leaned over her, his body hot and solid against her back. His mouth skimmed her ear, his breath fanning over the side of her neck. "You have to say the words," he whispered. "You have to tell me what you want."

Emma opened her mouth, ready to tell them exactly what she wanted. Her eyelids lifted and she found herself in the bathtub, submerged chest-deep, in lukewarm water. Back in the harsh, cold reality that was her life. Alone.

Slapping the water, Emma sat up and lifted herself out of the tub. More hot and bothered than when she got in, Emma crossed the room and opened her top dresser drawer. Inside she quickly found what she wanted. The new toy she'd purchased online—a deluxe, multispeed vibrator.

Unconscious of the water still dripping off her body, Emma laid down on the bed and spread her thighs. Already worked up, she took no time for teasing herself. She ran the rounded tip up and down her slit, once and then again, getting it slippery, before applying it right where she needed it most. Right at the top of her sex, directly over the swollen and greedy nub of her clit.

Flicking on the vibration at its base, she rocked her hips up, pressing it harder against her, letting the steady pulsations bring her to a quick and easy finish. Shaking, her orgasm tapering off with slowing tremors, Emma still felt unfulfilled and restless.

Her orgasm took the edge off the ache between her thighs, but did nothing to relieve the ache in her heart. Or the need to feel strong, male arms around her. Her orgasm only reminded her she was alone, wanting something she now knew she could have, but wasn't sure would be good for her in the long run.

Questions like "What if things got weird?" or "What would happen when the novelty of a ménage wore off?" ran unchecked through her mind. She wasn't sure she would survive if they gave her a taste of what they had to offer, then kicked her to the wayside. Being with Will and Paul would ruin her for all other men. She just knew it.

Now, she sat on the corner of her bed, her knees pulled up under her chin, staring at the clock above the dinette set, contemplating her next move. Paul had served the ball into her court. She could choose to hit it back, or let it bounce away untouched.

Was she brave enough to risk everything on the slim likelihood that she could end up with more than she'd ever dreamed possible? She felt like she was playing Russian roulette with her future.

If things went bad, she would have to move, find a new job, get away from the nosy, prying eyes and rumors that were bound to follow when she was dumped by yet another O'Malley brother, along with his lover. Could she dare take a chance on them?

Yes!

Her heart screamed for her to spin the wheel of chance. Her brain wasn't so sure, but damn it, she listened to her brain too much anyway. And where the hell had it ever gotten her? This time, she was going to go with her heart and hope for the best.

Emma glanced at the clock. It was almost midnight. Should she go now or wait till morning? *Do it now*, her conscience advised. *Go right now, before you lose your nerve and wuss out.*

She got up off the bed and stalked to her closet. It was late, but her men would still be up. They were bigger night owls than she was.

She was halfway through her wardrobe when she realized how she'd referred to Paul and Will. *Her men.* Damn, if that didn't have a nice ring to it.

Smiling a goofy smile, her nerves anxiously atwitter, she continued to scour her closet for something appropriate for seduction. If she was going to go through with this—and it appeared she was—she wanted to do it right.

* * *

After forcing some crackers and a cup of coffee into Paul in an effort to sober him up, Will paid their tab and dragged Paul out into the cool night air. Paul leaned heavily against him, his head propped up on Will's shoulder, and an arm thrown across his lower back.

Will hung onto Paul, slowly walking them in the direction of the back stairs that led to their apartment. Paul murmured and tried to pull away several times, only to stumble and sway before Will caught him and hoisted him up again.

By the time they rounded the back of the building, Will was swearing and sweating, even though it couldn't be more than sixty degrees outside, promising himself that it would be the last time he let either one of them drink outside the house. Somehow, he was always the one who ended up on babysitter duty.

He shoved Paul ahead of him at the bottom of the stairs, carefully following behind to make sure he didn't take an ass over teakettle fall back down the narrow steps. Bringing up the rear, Will watched Paul's ass sway from side to side as he clumsily maneuvered up the steps.

The view caused a lance of heat to rush to his groin. Will palmed his crotch, rearranging his cock as it stiffened to give it more room behind his fly.

With his gaze on Paul's ass, and his mind busy speculating whether or not Paul would stay awake long enough to take care of the hard-on he was causing, Will didn't pay any attention to their surroundings.

As they neared the top of the landing, Paul muttered something Will couldn't decipher. A split second later, Paul yelped and pitched forward.

Will's hand jabbed out, intent on grabbing Paul to prevent his fall, and fisted empty air, missing the back of Paul's shirt by mere inches.

Paul fell, landing with a muted thump and an oddly female squeak. The squeak startled Will. His gaze shot down, only then noticing the feminine form that had softened Paul's landing.

Softly curved, denim-clad legs, bent at the knee over the top step where she'd been sitting, were flanked on either side by Paul's thicker limbs. Shorter, feminine arms waved from under each side of Paul's chest. The curly black waterfall of hair cascading along the wood under Paul's shoulder identified the woman beneath him.

Emma.

If that hadn't already done the trick, her muffled "Help," from under Paul would have. Will would've recognized the husky pitch of her voice even from underwater.

Paul murmured an apology, or at least what sounded like one in his slurred, drunken accent, but didn't attempt to move off of her.

Will bent down and gripped Paul under the arms, grunting as he lifted his lover's substantial dead weight off of her.

His back braced against the railing behind him, Will held Paul up while Emma rose to her feet. The moon's iridescence kissed her features as she dusted herself off, slapping at the back of her tight jeans over her bottom and what she could reach of the back of the fitted black top. With every move, her breasts jiggled and pressed against the clingy fabric, outlining the firm cylindrical spheres and taut nipples.

Will's palms itched to feel their welcome weight.

She bent at the waist, both breasts shifting and pushing up in the deep V neckline of her shirt, as she swiped at the dust and bits of grass clinging to her calves.

It was clear by the way her breasts moved and shimmied that she wasn't wearing a bra. Only the thin fabric of her top stopped those puppies from bursting free and killing him. And kill him it would, because he would die if he was faced with the beautiful bounty of her tits and was unable to touch them and suck them like he hungered to.

He groaned. The thought of tasting her was too much for him to handle.

Emma looked up from what she was doing, and cocked an eyebrow at him in question. "You okay over there?"

That was one of the very things that drew him to her. She was so naïve when it came to her allure with the opposite sex. Seemingly blind to the beauty she possessed.

"I'm fine," Will lied. "Paul's just getting a little heavy."

Emma stepped back, pressing her back against the opposite side of the railing to clear his path to the door. "Sorry. I guess I was standing right in your way, huh?"

"Uh, yeah," Will mumbled, not knowing what else to say. The situation with Emma was an awkward one. He didn't know why she was there. Well, he did, but he didn't. She was obviously there because of the talk she'd had with Paul, but her answer to their proposal remained unseen.

Will felt like a coward, but he wasn't altogether sure he wanted to hear what she had to say. Either answer was going to change things. Whether the change would be for the better was yet to be determined.

Needing a hand free so that he could dig in his pocket for the house key, he shifted Paul's weight to one side. An evil thought occurred to him, and popped out of his mouth before he could refrain. "Emma, do you think you could help me out here? The house key's in my pocket, but I can't get to it and hold up Paul at the same time. Do you think you could get it out for me and unlock the door?"

Emma bit her lip, like she was prone to do when nervous, and nodded. Will wanted to kiss her; she looked so cute when she was flustered.

She stepped closer and touched his side gently, like he was a snake ready to strike her if she made any sudden moves. It was an apt thought, for when her fingers combed over his hip, searching for his pocket, he felt like jumping her. Or introducing her to the pet snake coiled in his trousers.

Gingerly, she felt around until she located the flap and slipped her dainty fingers inside. Will held his breath, his entire being concentrating on the feel of her fingertips brushing over him. The thin cotton lining was the only thing that stood between her touch and his yearning flesh.

Paul wiggled in his arms, distracting Will as Emma continued to rummage through his pocket.

He felt her hand fist, closing over something. Most likely the key, and then she began to pull it out. As she did, she brushed over the root of his cock, and Will thought he would have to bite his tongue in half to stifle his groan.

Paul, the devil that he was, chose that instant to push his ass back against Will. The move smashed Emma's hand into his groin and pinned it there, right above the head of his cock. Her quick, in-drawn breath assured Will that she'd noticed the swollen state of his dick.

Instead of jerking her hand away like he expected her to do, Emma pressed her breasts closer against his side, damn near plastering herself to him. Her hand opened and released the key, letting it fall back into the dredges with whatever the hell else he had in there. At that moment, he could have had an atom bomb in his pocket, and he wouldn't have known the difference. All he felt was her, brushing up against his side, and her fingers rubbing over his groin.

"Oops," she whispered with a chuckle that he could've sworn was the sexiest, raunchiest sound he'd ever heard in his life. "Dropped it." And then her fingers moved, rummaging around, touching and feeling everything but the key he'd asked her to find.

He cursed himself silently for shifting his dick to the left instead of the right after his last piss, because he just knew that it would be in her tiny hand otherwise.

Paul wiggled, pushing back against him yet again, and this time Will couldn't hold in the moan. Paul's ass punched Emma's wrist down over the hard-as-a-pike root of his cock. It didn't feel good. His prick could hammer nails, he was so hard, and having it prodded back into his stomach wasn't the greatest feeling.

The small spike of pain cleared his lust-fogged brain enough to draw in air, enabling him to speak. "Emma, Paul's getting a little hard to hold onto. Do you think you could hurry it up?" If she didn't, he was going to come the next time she inadvertently stroked him. A man could only take so much, for Christ's sake.

She made a small noise, barely loud enough for him to hear. "Sure. I'm trying to get it, but it's a slippery sucker."

Yeah, Will thought, *it wasn't the only thing getting slippery*. He was oozing enough pre-come to lube a fleet of jet engines.

Emma latched onto the key. "Got it," she said, pulling her fist free of his pocket and holding it out for inspection.

"Thanks, Emma. Would you mind getting the door?" he replied, shifting Paul up before the wiggly bastard slipped out of his grip.

When Emma turned her attention to the door, Will kneed Paul in the ass. Paul grunted, but otherwise didn't make a peep. Will didn't think Paul was quite as drunk as he was playing, but now wasn't the time to point it out. He could get even with Paul after Emma had said her peace and left.

Emma pushed the door inward, and held the screen out for them to pass. A stickler for gentlemanly behavior, Will nodded toward the open door and waited for her to go in ahead of them.

Chapter Seven

Will was hard pressed not to start banging his head on the wall. As he'd suspected, Paul wasn't nearly as toasted as he'd pretended to be. The moment Will walked him through the bedroom door and pulled it shut behind them, Paul brushed off his hands and burst out laughing.

Will didn't know whether to strangle him or pull his own hair out. He settled on promising retribution for the morning and left the room, leaving Paul sitting on the side of the bed, fighting clumsily to untie his sneakers.

Will closed the door behind him, pausing for a moment to get his Bearings before walking down the hall. Emma was waiting for him in the living room.

The closer each step brought him to where he'd left her sitting on the couch, the deeper he felt the line between his brows etching into his forehead. The beginnings of a headache built behind his eyes and made them sting.

He really didn't want to deal with any of this mess tonight. Will started to understand why an ostrich buried its head in the sand. His uncertainty over the future, over Emma and Paul, was enough to make him envy the huge bird for its ability to hide.

Will pasted a strained smile on his face and marched over to where Emma sat, her back turned to him, on the corner of the beige leather sofa.

His eyes softened as he took a quick glance at her, the muted light from the single lamp falling over the dark riot of curls skimming her shoulders and the hands clasped tightly in her lap. He couldn't help noticing the nervous way she twisted her fingers and pressed her thumbs together.

Damn if she wasn't adorable. Here she was, probably getting ready to tear him a new one, and *she* was nervous.

Will cleared his throat, alerting her to his presence, before moving around her to sit on the opposite side of the couch. The side farthest from the illuminated lamp Emma sat beside. He hoped the shadows that fell over his head would mask any emotion he wouldn't be able to hide from her as they talked.

"So," Will coughed into his hand. "What brings you by so late tonight?"

Emma blushed, adding a cute splash of pink to the apple of each of her cheeks. "I...um...wanted to talk to Paul."

What was he supposed to say to that? She didn't know Paul had already spilled the beans to him. The man couldn't keep a secret if his ass depended on it. *Better not to mention it until she did.* "Well, you're welcome to try, but I don't think you're going to get him to say anything that makes sense tonight. You'll have to come back in the morning, when he's more...alert."

"*No!* No, that's okay. I mean. Damn," she said, followed by a nervous little twitter of laughter, "I'm not doing this very well. Paul and I had a talk this afternoon. He told me some things, and I just wanted to—"

"Paul told me," Will interjected, hoping to save her a long and tedious explanation that would no doubt be uncomfortable for the both of them. *So much for keeping his big mouth shut.*

Her beautiful blue eyes widened a fraction, and the pink tinge to her cheeks kicked up a notch on the pigment scale. "Oh. I...um..."

Watching Emma prattle was about the cutest thing he'd ever seen, but he decided to show her some mercy. "No reason to be bashful, Emma. How long have we known each other—something like six or seven years? If you want me to relay a message to Paul, telling him to stick his crazy idea up his ass, then that's what I'll do."

"Oh. No, that's not what I—"

Will sighed. "It's no problem, Emma." He ran a hand through his hair, briefly making a note to himself to get a cut. When his hair started to curl on the ends and tangle around his fingers, the way it was now, he was way past due on a visit to the barbershop.

Okay, so he was trying to think about anything but the confused look on Emma's face. Who the hell could blame him? If he started trying to figure out the inner workings of the female mind, he would lose his. Some things were better left alone. He could easily spend the next fifty years trying to figure out whether the disappointed shadow lurking behind her eyes was really there, or just his own wishful thinking. *Nope, he wasn't going to go there.*

Will perched on the edge of the sofa. He'd let Emma off the hook, so to speak. Any minute now, he expected to be following her to the front door and watching her hasty exit. Not a moment too soon either, because the scent of her perfume, or wherever the sweet smell of honeysuckle came from, was driving him crazy. It made him salivate for a taste of what he clearly wasn't ever going to get. Would it be asking too much for one long lick of the delicious treats she flaunted under the painted-on outfit she wore? *Probably. Damn it.*

Will, as inconspicuously as possible, shifted his needy penis before he rose to his feet. Standing over Emma was a whole new level of torture. He could see right down her blouse. The open V-neck provided just a big enough glimpse of cleavage to make his tongue itch.

If she'd gone braless to torment him, it was working. He couldn't tear his eyes away from her breasts. Even when he felt her gaze boring into him, noticing where he was looking, he couldn't stop. Her breasts, and the superimposed image of his dick sliding between them, held him captivated where he stood.

The breasts jiggled. That was how he knew Emma was moving, but nothing else registered. His eyes were locked on those ample, swelling breasts as they jostled and swayed. He was mesmerized by the ripe little nipples straining against the fabric, begging him to take them out and play with them, or suck on them to his heart's content.

"Will?"

He didn't answer, didn't look up. He didn't want to see the look of frustration marring her features. Or the anger he was sure would radiate from her eyes. If he was going to get slapped for ogling her, then he was damn sure going to make it worth his while.

The sting of her palm against his face never came. Instead both of her open hands landed on his chest and pushed. The unexpected shove landed Will right back where he'd started—on his ass toward the dark corner of the couch. The back of his skull thunked off the top hard edge of the couch frame.

The pain blossoming in his head was the last thing he felt as Emma climbed up on his lap and straddled his thighs. What was a little headache when his dick was so hard it was on the verge of splitting in half like an overcooked wiener?

His gaze flew up to Emma's face. Her expression clouded by shadows, he could barely make out the tip of her tongue swiping over her lips. Her hands landed on his shoulders, bracing her weight, and then her lips descended on his, rubbing, caressing, nipping at him, as if he were her last meal and she planned to savor it.

Will closed his eyes, parted his lips, and kissed back. His arms rose to wrap around the small of her back. Both hands cradled the rise of her bottom and pulled her tighter against him.

He slanted his head for a better fit against her small cupid's-bow mouth, and thrust his tongue into her mouth, moving against her in a frantic parry of lovers long denied their addiction. A low, starved moan echoed in his ears. Will wasn't sure who it came from, him or her, and he didn't care.

Emma shifted, her hips rotating over his groin, pressing down into his lap. Behind the steel cage of his zipper, his cock ached and throbbed to be set free. Just a few layers of clothes to be removed or pushed aside and he could be inside her, making love to her, like he'd dreamed of doing for so damn long.

He pulled his mouth from hers, inhaling much needed oxygen before running his lips over her jaw and down her neck, tasting the ambrosia of her skin.

Small, breathy whimpers spilled from Emma's throat, egging him on. They told him that she liked what he was doing. Will pulled at the neck of her top, revealing the curve of her throat and collarbone to his seeking mouth. Busy sucking and nipping at the skin he'd discovered, Will felt Emma's hands on his chest, but didn't think much of it until cool air washed over him, quickly followed by the heat of her palms gliding over his pecs, squeezing his nipples, and trailing down his stomach toward the clasp of his pants.

He lifted his head to tell her to stop, but any protests he had were scattered to the wind and swallowed by her lips swooping down to claim his. Emma pulled his tongue into her mouth, sucked on it, and Will snapped. His control in tatters, he rose off the couch and flipped them.

Emma landed on her back atop the wide couch. Will followed her down, one elbow coming to rest on either side of her shoulders.

His hand fisted in the stretchy fabric of her top and yanked, pulling the flexible material down under her heaving breasts. Emma's gasp in response to his action and their matched struggle for oxygen were the only sounds in the quiet room.

Will stared, devastated by the sheer luminescence of her beauty. Her breasts were the palest of creams, round and full, topped by tightly puckered cotton candy pink nipples that begged to be ravished. He bent his head and obliged their call, his tongue flicking out to lave one and then the other.

Emma's back arched, pushing her nipple deeper into his mouth. "Will. Oh, God. Yes, please." Her hands rose, fisting in his hair, tugging him closer.

Ultimately, it was the sound of her passion that pulled him back to reality. His name, falling so musically from her lush lips, caused him to glance up.

In their new position, dim light cast by the lamp washed over them. A halo of light surrounded Emma's face and shoulders like a divine intervention for a dark angel. Will saw Emma, took in her flushed cheeks, the sheen of moisture on her parted, kiss-swollen lips, and the lacy curve of ebony lashes resting against her pearlescent skin.

His brother's image appeared, like a ghastly specter in his mind's eye, and Will pulled back, scooting away from Emma to the farthest edge of the couch.

He raked a rough paw through his mangled hair and cursed. What the hell where they doing? This was wrong. She was his kid brother's ex. More than that, he had a lover lying asleep down the hall. He couldn't let her get involved in the mess that was his life. She was too sweet, too innocent, to withstand the backlash being in an unorthodox relationship would cause. He must have fucking lost his mind to let things get as far as they had.

Emma sat up beside him, righting her top, before laying a hand on his shoulder. "Are you okay? What's the matter?"

"I'm sorry. I can't do this."

"What? But I thought…" Her voice trailed off into nothing. The couch cushions shifted as she stood up. "Paul said that you—"

Will looked up, his elbows on his knees, his chin resting in his open hands. "I said no, Emma. This won't work!"

Emma flinched. She took a step back, her hand fluttering up to her throat like a wounded bird. "If you weren't interested," she whispered, her eyes refusing to meet his, "all you had to do was say so." She pivoted on one heel and stalked toward the door.

Will caught the sheen of tears in her eyes as she turned. He had only a second to make his decision—should he go after her or let her go, knowing full well that his big mouth was the cause of her tears—and then he was up off the sofa and hurrying after her.

His hand landed on the apple of her shoulder. "Emma, wait."

She twisted away from him. "Leave me alone."

"I'm sorry, Emma. I'm an ass," Will said to the back of her head since she wouldn't turn around to look at him.

She snuffled and hiccupped. "What do you want from me, Will? One minute you're all over me, and the next you're acting like a scared virgin on prom night. I don't get it. I thought…"

She snuffled again and Will couldn't resist pulling her into his arms. She tried to resist, but he wouldn't have it. He pulled her back against his chest and held onto her, his cheek resting on the top of her head. The sweet scent that was all

Emma wafted up from her hair and intoxicated him. "You thought what?"

"It doesn't matter."

"It does to me," he whispered into her ear. He ran his hands up and down her arms, trying to soothe her. "I didn't mean to upset you. Sometimes I open my mouth and things come out the wrong way. I didn't mean to growl at you."

His fingertips inadvertently brushed the sides of her breasts. Emma trembled in his arms. "I just want to know what's going on, Will. Paul implied a lot of different things this afternoon. Things I had some trouble dealing with—at first—but then I decide to go for it, to take a chance. And I come here, ready to open myself to the possibilities and..." She shook her head slightly and turned, her eyes sparkling with moisture as she stared up at him. "Now you're confusing the hell out of me. What is it you want? Do you want me, Will? If you do, say so now, because after I walk out that door, you're never going to get another chance. It's now or never."

Chapter Eight

Emma stared up into Will's deep brown eyes, and prayed he wouldn't reject her. Blood thrummed through her veins and caused her heartbeat to echo loudly in her ears as she waited to hear what he was going to say.

The steel set of his square jaw and the tense line of his wide shoulders didn't bode well for her. She absently noted the way his fists clenched and unclenched at his sides. Was that because he was having trouble keeping his hands to himself, or because he wanted to strangle her for her audacity?

She couldn't believe she'd issued him an ultimatum, but she knew if he rebuffed her advances tonight, she wouldn't have the balls to come back. Rejection was a sore spot with her, and she wasn't going to let him keep prodding it with a stick while he made up his mind.

The silence between them grew thick, filling the air with tension. She wanted to raise her hand and wipe away the worry lines that creased Will's forehead, but didn't feel it was her right or place to do it. She wished Paul was there, able to act as a soothing buffer between them.

Emma found it strange that she could wish for another's presence, when it was Will her body throbbed for ever since that first kiss on the sofa. If she could call the way he'd ravaged her lips and set her aflame something as simple as a kiss. The ease with which he'd taken over, taken control of their passion and drove it higher, blew her mind. If he could make her need him so much after nothing more than a teenage grope-fest, what would it be like to unleash all his hunger, to get him naked and feel the full force of his desire?

And that wasn't even taking into account Paul and his needs.

Emma shuddered under the desire to find out what it would be like to be loved by them both. Will was her focus and she needed to concentrate on what was happening right now, not on the possibilities of what could happen in the future. If Will turned her away, she wouldn't have to worry about it anyhow.

"Emma, I..."

Oh, here it comes. The expression on his face was too self-defeating for him to have anything good to say.

Emma stiffened her spine, standing a wee bit taller, her posture a tad more straight. No matter what he decided, she resolved to walk out of the apartment with her head held high. She could act like a reasonable adult for the amount of time it took her to get home. Once she got there though, all bets were off.

"So, are we going to fuck, or what?" This came from Paul, as he rounded the corner of the hallway and stepped into the living room behind Will.

Emma swallowed a snicker. Leave it to Paul to break the tension. The man was adorable; all tousled blond hair and mischievous green eyes. The fact that he was damn near naked, clad in only a pair of hilarious black silk boxers with roosters printed all over them, didn't hurt either.

She glanced up at Will, who was busy looking back over his shoulder at Paul, and kept her mouth shut. It was up to Will to decide what happened next.

* * *

Paul was an impatient bastard. He would be the first to admit it. Having to lie back in the bedroom, his hand stroking his cock, while he waited on Emma and Will to "have their moment" had almost killed him.

He'd given them as much time alone as he could stand. Considering the steel quality of his hard-on, they were lucky to have gotten what they did.

He'd hoped to find them locked together in a passionate embrace into which he could easily insinuate himself. What he'd found—the two of them locking horns two steps from the front door—hadn't been anywhere near what he'd had in mind. Even before he'd caught a glimpse of Emma's gloomy eyes, the tight cast to Will's shoulders told him all was not going well.

It didn't take a stretch of the imagination to figure out why. Emma was there and obviously willing. That left Will. Paul was sure the tension he felt was one of two things; either Will was suffering from a case of stage fright, or he'd blurted out something and hurt her feelings.

Will was a big teddy Bear on most occasions, but the man did have a way of sticking his foot in his mouth at the worst times.

That was okay though. Paul would straighten it out for him. He loved the big lug, so he didn't mind soothing the toes Will occasionally trampled over. That's what partners did. When one screwed up, the other stepped in to help. He'd certainly stomped enough feelings himself with his tendency toward poking fun at everything.

Their meeting on the stairs outside, for instance. He'd thought it was hilarious when Emma began teasing Will. Shoving back into the man, forcing them into closer proximity, seemed like a good idea. Kind of like waving a red flag at a bull. Will probably didn't think so. Hell, Will had most likely thought Emma was accidentally touching his dick.

Sometimes the man really was too blind for his own good. Will didn't see what was so obvious to anyone else looking in on the same situation. He was too busy letting his misplaced sense of "right and wrong" stand in the way of what he wanted.

Paul wasn't such a stickler. In his family, dysfunctional though it was, you went after what you wanted until you got it. Paul learned early on to take what he wanted from life because it wasn't going to be handed out on a silver platter.

He fully intended to keep pushing things along until Will opened his eyes and saw what was right in front of him. They had the opportunity to have something special. He would be damned before he let Will flush it down the toilet just because he was worried about the indefinable "ifs" that loomed somewhere down the road.

When his first attempt at cutting the ice didn't bring forth the response he wanted—or any response for that matter—he tried again. "So," he said, striding closer to the pair, "how do you feel about blowjobs, Emma? Spit or swallow?"

Will glared at him, practically vibrating annoyance.

Emma sighed and backed away from Will. Her eyes slowly met Paul's. "Doesn't matter, Will isn't interested." Her gaze shot to Will, as if daring him to say differently. When he didn't, she looked down at her watch. "I have to go." She waved her hand and laughed hollowly. "Things to do and all."

She turned and pulled open the door.

"Emma, wait!" Paul hollered.

She shook her head and walked out the door. The screen banged back against the frame, loud as a gunshot in the quiet room.

Paul dropped a hand on Will's arm. "Way to go, meathead. Why didn't you stop her? All she wanted was for you to admit your feelings for her."

Will rounded on Paul. "You are *not* going to blame this on me! This whole ridiculous idea was yours. I never agreed to anything." He snatched his arm out of Paul's grip. "You just went along your merry way and talked to her without even considering the ramifications."

Paul swaggered over to the sofa and flopped down, suddenly exhausted with the whole thing. You could force a horse to water, but you couldn't make the damn thing drink. Although in this case, Will resembled a jackass more than a horse.

"And what precisely would the ramifications be? Would the earth stop revolving around the sun, or the oceans rise up and swallow us whole? Give me a break. Just admit that you were too big a pussy to tell the woman you're in love with her."

"I never said I was in love with her. And why the hell do you care anyway? Haven't you screwed up enough for me?"

Paul swallowed down the bitter taste of bile creeping up the back of his throat. He couldn't manage to contain the deep ingrained hurt and anger Will's hastily spewed words caused. "What is that supposed to mean?" He stood and quickly crossed the room until he stood in front of Will. "I've fucked up your life, huh? I don't remember forcing my dick into your mouth, and I sure as hell don't recall forcing you to like it so damn much."

Will blanched. He blew out hot air and his chest seemed to deflate right before Paul's eyes. Irritation and misguided anger drained right out of Will, along with the carbon dioxide. "Fuck, baby, I'm sorry. I didn't mean that." He shook his head. "I just don't know what to do. Things are so fucked up. One minute everything was fine, I was kissing her and things were going good—so damn, unbelievably good—then Mark popped into my head and everything went to hell."

Feeling gracious, Paul decided to let Will's outburst slide. They could have a nice long talk about those old issues creeping in later. After they resolved the current issue on the table. "You go after her. That's what you do."

"But what if—"

"No. No what ifs! Stop worrying about what your damn brother is going to think, and go after Emma. Tell her how you feel, or you're going to regret it. We both will."

"Are you sure about this, Paul?"

Paul pressed a quick kiss to Will's closed lips. He pointed to the door and the keys that hung suspended on a hook right next to it. "Go. I want you to."

Chapter Nine

Emma had just enough time to get inside her apartment, add a bra to her outfit because she wasn't about to go in public without one, and stalk across the room before she heard the distinctive purr of a motorcycle. Footsteps thumped their way up her stairs, followed by a fist banging on the front door. She gave up on the idea of going out for a beer, and headed back to the door.

She wasn't stupid. She knew it was Paul. He'd come to let her down easy, and apologize for Will's being an ass. The man really was too sweet for words. It was a shame she wasn't going to be able to have much to do with him any longer. A gal could only take so much humiliation. Throwing herself at a gay man—what the hell had she been thinking?

Emma yanked open the door—ready to blast Paul for his dumbass idea, and the fact that he had driven over without being entirely sober—and stopped.

Not Paul.

Will's lean cheeks were flushed red, his hair wind-tousled from the ride over. The front of his shirt gaped open, just the way it had when she'd left. She couldn't help but recall how her fingers worked those tiny buttons open, and bared him inch by inch, clear to his navel.

Through the sparse smatter of hair on his chest, she noticed his puckered nipples. That made her think of her own breasts, and how hot and wet his tongue had felt running over them. Her womb clenched, desire sliding down her passage and moistening the cotton lining on her panties.

Her body's innate response to him pissed her off. She clenched her teeth, and sucked in a deep breath through her nose. She was not going to melt for this man. She *wasn't.* Only a masochist would give him a second chance to spurn her.

She started to slam the door in his face, but curiosity got the better of her. "What are you doing here?"

Will stepped forward, his large bulk forcing her to step back. "We need to talk."

Emma allowed Will to maneuver his way inside her small living quarters. His boot kicked the door shut behind him, sealing them in together. His large presence made her tiny home seem even smaller, approximately the size of a doll house.

Did that make her plus-size Barbie? Psh, as if there were such a thing.

Her back hit the wall, leaving her nowhere to go when Will sidled up in front of her. He stopped a hairsbreadth away, so close his humid breath fanned the tip of her nose. The enticing smell of him, all hot musk and faint cologne, enveloped her like a hug.

A tremor zigzagged down her spine and split into each leg. Her thighs shook, and her knees turned to jelly. "What...what do you think you're doing?" The sound of her voice surprised her. It was much too high pitched.

"I'm setting the record straight."

Her eyes felt huge and dry because she refused to blink, or take her eyes off him for a single second. "Huh?" *How was she supposed to think straight with his mouth so close, his heat wrapping her in a fog of want?*

He grabbed her hand and brought it to his groin, pressing her palm over the hefty bulge beneath his pants. Her fingers automatically curved inward, wrapping around his swollen cock. It seemed to grow longer, harder, within her grasp.

His eyelids lowered, growing heavy, right along with his respiration. When he spoke, his voice was deep and rough, like starter fluid for her already raging libido. "Does that feel like I don't want you, Emma?"

His cock pulsed under her fingertips. Even through the layers of clothing, she could feel the hard stalk of his penis quiver with need, seemingly begging to be set free of its prison and petted, fawned over.

When she realized she was still caressing his tumescent length, Emma pulled her hand away, flinging it back to her side where it belonged. *Bad hand, bad!* "What do you want from me, Will?"

"Everything."

His lips descended, closing the small space between them, and covering her mouth in firm, soft skin just asking to be nipped and tasted in return.

Emma fought not to be consumed by his kiss, tried to resist the lure of falling into his embrace, and lost the battle.

Strong arms wrapped around her. Will licked the seam between her closed lips, seeking entrance. His hands cupped her bottom, and raised her onto her toes. At the same time, his fingers kneaded her flesh, causing her to moan. He took the inch he'd gained and a mile more, ravaging the fragile depths of her mouth with his tongue, gliding it over and alongside hers.

Emma broke. She kissed back, conveying all her passion and her need through the meeting of lips and mouths. She nipped at his bottom lip, pulled it into her mouth and sucked.

Will groaned into her mouth and Emma swallowed it, relishing his response. He shifted closer, pressing her harder against the wall, and grinded his groin into hers, letting her feel his desire for her.

Her hands dropped to his pants, fingers fumbling to undo the buttons. The last one stuck, refusing to open and she swore soundlessly. *The hell with it.* She ripped the flap open and yanked down, trying to make room for her hands to slide inside. Instead of boxers, she encountered smooth, heated flesh. She twisted her hand inside, wrapped around the base of his penis and pulled the heavy length through the gap, freeing him to her touch.

Hard and ready, his cock hung out of the front of his pants, weighed down by the sheer mass of his girth. Her fist weighed and cupped him, running up and down his impressive length before sliding inside his pants to cup the heavy, wrinkled sac beneath.

This time, she was getting her fill. He could pull away at any time, change his mind and leave her hanging, again.

Before that could happen, she was going to quench her curiosity about the body she'd been lusting after for years, and see and taste the sex of the man she wanted to make love to more than she wanted to live to old age and die surrounded by precocious grandchildren.

Twisting her face to the side, she broke free of their kiss and dropped to her knees.

One of Will's hands fisted in her hair, stilling her forward progression. "Emma, don't—"

She pressed on, ignoring the pull of her hair. *Oh, God.* His cock was right there in front of her face, long and hard and thick, just as she'd dreamed it would be. She wouldn't be denied, not now, not when she was so close to fulfilling her fantasy.

She wrapped her fingers around the base of his penis, surprised when they didn't meet around his enormous girth, and pulled it toward her. A clear bead of moisture lay in the middle of the wide, round head, clinging to small slit like a refreshing drop of rain. Her tongue flicked out, laving over the tip and taking with it a small taste of his essence. Salty and delicious, she wanted more. She leaned in closer and ran the tip of her tongue over the protruding vein that began under the shallow groove of his cockhead and followed it down his shaft. She traced the soft, firm flesh all the way down to where it connected to the smoother, more delicate skin covering the fragile orbs of his testicles. One at a time, she sucked them into her mouth, her tongue rasping over the sensitive sex organs.

Will groaned, his hand fisting tighter in her hair. His other hand roamed down the side of her face, whispered over her cheek. "Oh, Emma. Stop baby, I'm too close."

Voracious in her hunger for him, she ignored his request and moved higher, sucking the tip of his cock into her mouth. Her cheeks hollowed as she took all of him that she could inside her mouth and sucked. Enough of him remained outside of her mouth to occupy both hands. She fisted them one atop the other, twisting and pulling in tempo with each long draw of suction up and down the first several inches of his shaft.

She felt his heartbeat through the heated flesh in her mouth and under her exploring tongue. It grew faster as his penis throbbed under her tender ministrations. Twinges of electricity shot from her clit into her pussy, making her clench emptily and yearn to be filled by him.

She took one hand off his penis, and worked at the snap on her jeans, desperate for some stimulation on her overheated sex. The zipper caught, refusing to slide down, and she whimpered piteously around his flesh, frantic for relief from the insistent ache deep inside her core.

From under her lashes, she glanced up at Will. His head was tilted back, eyes squeezed shut, his lips parted as he drew in ragged gulps of air. As if he felt her gaze on him, his face lowered and he opened his eyes, the normal deep chocolate color now black with ardor.

They stared at one another as her mouth continued up and down his length, leaving the rigid staff slick and shiny in her wake.

Will shuddered, his big body trembling with desire. He bent at the waist, his hands seizing her under the arms and lifting. Despite the mutinous look she tired to give him, he pulled her away from her pleasurable task and up onto her feet.

He gripped the zipper on her pants and tugged, ripping it from the seams. Emma gasped.

Will worked her jeans over her hips and down her legs. He squatted in front of her and slipped off her shoes, tossing them aside. While he removed her pants, one leg and the other, Emma pulled her shirt over her head, gave it a fling, and unclasped the front catch on her bra. She shrugged the uncomfortable garment off her shoulders and dropped it, laughing when one of the cups landed on Will's head, the straps hanging precariously off to each side.

He yanked her pants the rest of the way off, his eyes blazing up at her. "Think that's funny, do you?" he growled, pulling the bra off his head.

Emma nodded, too choked up to speak.

He rose to his feet, towering over her by half a foot. While she was down to a pair of sheer black high-cut satin panties, he was still fully dressed. Not a single piece missing, they were all just skewed, hanging open to frame the sexy planes and angles of his masculine form.

She started to push the shirt off his back, set on equaling their nakedness, when he grabbed her wrists and stopped her. One big paw held both her slender wrists captive while the other twined her bra around them, binding them together.

She tugged against the knot, testing it and encountered no give in the binding. She trusted Will, but that didn't stop the equal shots of nervousness and excitement that fought for dominance in her system. "Will? What are you doing?"

"Making sure you can't get away from me again," he replied, raising her hands above her head and twisting the bra over a plant hanger that stuck out from the wall above her.

He moved back and regarded her with hot eyes. "That should just about do it."

Emma gulped. "Just about?"

"Mm hmm." He dropped down on his knees. "I think you'll be more comfortable without these," he said as his fingers slid under the elastic of her panties, and began to work them off. He leaned back on his heels and stared. "Perfect."

Naked as the day she was born, Emma stared down at Will. The cool air in the open room washed over her skin, causing goose bumps to rise all over her body. Her nipples drew up into tight beads, though whether that was from the chill or the flush of nerves from being tied up and at Will's mercy, she wasn't sure.

Will's knuckles brushed over the strip of trimmed hair covering her mons, and then the bare lips of her sex. His thumb slipped inside her layers and teased the erect bud of clit.

Hot air blew over the moist petals of her sex. The chill was quickly replaced with the heat of his mouth. His tongue swiped through her folds, exploring her every rise and hollow. Firm lips tugged softly on her labia. The tip of his pointed tongue searched out her clit, and teased over it before he pulled the small kernel into his mouth and sucked.

Emma's head fell back, softly banging against the wall. She didn't notice or care about the impact; her entire world revolved around Will's touch and how it made her melt.

Her breasts grew heavy, nipples seeming to vibrate with need. She wanted him to touch them, to play with them like he had earlier. What he was doing was great—damn great—but she needed more. She didn't want to reach climax without him. Emma wanted Will with her when she came.

"Will," she moaned, her arms pulling at her bindings. "Stop. I need you to…" *fuck me.* Her face heated at the words in her mind. Here she was, naked and trussed up, but couldn't manage to tell him what she wanted. She was too embarrassed to put her needs into words.

"What do you need, Emma?"

She kept her eyes squeezed closed, not wanting to face him, not wanting him to see the desperate hunger she felt clawing at her insides through her gaze. "You," she whispered. "I need you…inside me."

A growl rumbled from Will, causing her to look down at him. His eyes flared up at her in return.

Will gave her needy sex one last flick of his tongue and rose to his feet. She watched, her eyelids heavy, as he tore off his clothes. Finally, naked, he came to her. All hard muscle and brawn, his body was a work of art. His huge penis seemed to lead the way, jutting out of its wreath of silky curls.

Emma licked her lips, remembering the addictive taste of his tumescent flesh. The way she'd felt so powerful, so in charge of her femininity, while she was in control of his desire.

Will groaned, his eyes on her mouth, and she did it again just to torment him.

"Enough," he murmured. His calloused hands gripped her hips, his fingers digging into the soft padding on her backside and lifted, raising her off her feet with little apparent effort.

Emma wrapped her legs around his waist, locking her ankles behind his back, and held on as best she could. Higher, she was able to strain up and lift her brassiere handcuffs over the hook and bring her arms down around Will's neck. She buried her fingers in the thick hair at Will's nape and pulled his lips down to hers.

Will's tongue plunged into her mouth at the same time his penis forged into her channel, stretching the delicate tissues of her sex wide around his incredible girth.

"Oh God, Will," she cried out, her head tilting back and her eyelids slamming down. The feel of Will inside her was too much. No, it wasn't enough. She needed friction.

As if he read her mind, Will began to move. His first thrusts were long and slow, giving her much needed time to adjust to his invasion of her body. Gradually, he built up his pace until he was slamming the entire length of his engorged cock in and out, over and over again.

The wreath of hair around his sex ground into her mound, tantalizing her clit with every downward lunge, driving her higher, closer to the pinnacle she strained to reach.

Will shifted, changing the angle of his thrust, and began to hit something deep inside her tunnel that had never been touched before. Tension coiled in her stomach, winding ever tighter. "Yes! Oh God, Will, don't stop! Harder."

"Emma! Oh fuck, baby, I'm close. Come for me."

Will's cock expanded inside her, pulsing with life, and tipped her over the edge. Emma screamed, her climax barreling through her with the strength of a hurricane.

From deep inside the void of release, she heard Will cry out, her name pouring from his lips as he tumbled over the precipice with her.

Chapter Ten

Warm. Emma felt warm and safe and damned comfortable.

A fluffy pillow was beneath her head, neither too soft nor too thick. The fleece blanket around her body infused her with warmth, and slid over her skin like butter. Chill air swished around her face, making her much more determined not to open her eyes and fully awaken.

The bed shifted, jostling her closer to consciousness, and she moaned piteously. Just a few more minutes of sleep, long enough to see a little more of the delicious dream she was having about Will taking her against the wall. Then she would get up. *She swore she would.*

Emma burrowed deeper under the covers, trying to get away from the cool air and bright light trying its best to interrupt her rest. Fuzzy images of going down on Will, and of him returning the favor, played on a loop in her head.

Nimble fingers slid down her abdomen, and trailed over the soft curls of her mound. Her path unobstructed by panties, she slid the pad of one fingertip along her slit, teasing her body, pretending it was Will's tongue as she replayed the image of Will on his knees licking her, sucking at her as if he couldn't get enough of the honey her body was producing for him.

Low whispers permeated her consciousness. She dismissed them—thinking she must have fallen asleep with the TV on again—and continued pleasuring herself in the hazy fog of half-sleep.

She imagined hands on her thighs, separating them. A warm, firm set of lips nudging her fingers out of the way, swiping over her swollen folds and delving into the moist interior between them. The very tip feathered over her erect clit, and Emma sucked in air, holding it as the familiar spiraling tension of an approaching orgasm started in the pit of her stomach and spread languorously through her body.

Her nipples puckered and throbbed. Emma raised one hand and tugged at her nipples, trying to soothe the ache in her breasts.

So close to detonation, she moaned. Her hips arched, pushing up off the bed, and just like that she toppled over the edge, her cunt spasming in climax.

Never in her life had she experienced such a realistic dream. It was almost as if…

A strong arm wrapped around her waist, pulling her back against a hair-roughened chest. A second one slid underneath her back and around to her front, cupping one of her breasts. She could feel a hard morning erection pressing into her bottom. Firm, moist lips nuzzled her neck from behind.

"Good morning." Will's deep voice rumbled against the curve of her neck.

She sighed and pushed back into him, relishing the feel of his powerful body against hers.

Prickly morning stubble brushed over her slick labial lips, pulling her further from the murkiness of sleep. Emma's eyes flew open. Her hands frantically threw aside the cover.

Paul stared back at her, a mischievous twinkle in his heavily lidded, sexy green eyes. "Good morning, Kitten."

The previous night's events rushed back to her. Will's making love to her against the wall wasn't a realistic dream. It had happened. As had his bribing her into coming home with him afterwards. The conniving fool had threatened to spend the night with her if she didn't come home with him. Knowing what a disaster it would be for his motorcycle to stay parked in her driveway overnight, she'd easily given in.

By the time they'd arrived at his apartment, Paul had been fast asleep. She felt a little odd, getting into bed between two men—one of whom she'd just been intimate with, and the other who wasn't even aware of her presence—but she'd done it all the same. As her mom always said: in for a penny, in for a pound. She swallowed down the caginess she felt and climbed aboard.

Surprisingly, once ensconced in Will's arms, her back to his front, she drifted right off to sleep.

Waking up, however, with Paul's face between her thighs and Will plastered against her backside, was a little more disconcerting. Or it had been, until Will reached down and lifted her thigh over his, the bulbous head of his erection rubbing over and between her labia.

She moaned, pushing her ass back against him at just the right second, forcing the tip of his erection inside her. Will growled into her ear. He lifted her thigh higher and pressed deeper, burying his thick length to the hilt in one hard lunge.

Paul swung his lanky body around until he and Emma were in a sideways sixty-nine position. His face centered over her sex, the hard, throbbing length of his penis bouncing, slapping against the steel surface of his groin beneath his navel as he settled himself comfortably.

Emma reached out, running her fingers over the silky skin of his lengthy erection, and down to the tight wrinkled sac beneath, testing and marveling at the contrasts in texture.

She gripped the base of his penis, gliding her hand up and over the tip. Using the moisture she collected, Emma stroked the turgid length, back and forth, over and over. Her tongue flicked out to taste the silken pouch that held the essence of his manhood.

Paul groaned against her mound. The vibration sent wonderful, wicked sensations straight to her core.

His response compelled her to do more. With her tongue, she followed the shallow line bisecting his balls. When she reached the base of his penis, she began licking him with short, wet flicks, tonguing his shaft until she reached the flared ridge of his head.

Shifting her upper body forward, Emma tightened her hand around his shaft and swallowed as much of his cock as she could. She moved her mouth up and down, swiping her tongue into the shallow impression underneath the head where she knew he felt the most sensation.

His long prehensile tongue swiped through her folds, tickling slightly above the center of her pleasure, before moving down to rasp over where she and Will were so intimately joined. Emma closed her eyes, wallowing in the foreign but delicious feel of Will buried deep inside her and Paul's mouth fighting to bring her pleasure simultaneously. Her cunt felt stretched to its limits around Will's thick, invading cock, while Paul lapped at her pussy from the outside, stimulating every inch of her receptive flesh.

She lost the feel of Paul's wondering tongue at nearly the same time Will stiffened behind her. He cried out, "Oh, fuck, yeah," and shoved his hips harder against her, grinding his body into hers. Wet, smacking lips and slurping sounds reached her ears, and she knew Paul must have been doing something exquisite to Will just out of her range of view.

Her eyes flicked up to the ceiling, and the plain white plaster finish. She would have to do something about that. A mirror would work wonders above the bed. It would be sexy as hell to watch the three of them while they made love.

Will began to thrust his hips. Long, slow plunges caused her back to arch into him, and her mouth fell open as indecipherable, garbled pleas escaped.

Paul's tongue gently brushed over her swollen, sensitive pussy. Each pass of his agile tongue over her clit sent tiny bolts of electricity surging through her, leaving her entire body feeling like a conduit for the two men loving her so thoroughly.

Will pinched her nipple between his thumb and forefinger. The small bite of pain sent a fresh deluge of moisture into her already saturated channel. He did it again, squeezing harder, and her tightly stretched muscles clenched, making him moan against her neck and shuttle his huge cock deeper, faster, into her pliable body.

Emma moaned around Paul's rigid cock, taking him further into her mouth. His cockhead hit the back of her throat. Her gag reflex flared to life, making her eyes water and her throat burn. She pinched her eyes shut and pressed on, determined to show Paul as much pleasure as both he and Will were showing her.

His hips arched, butting his penis against her tonsils, and instinct made her swallow. Her eyes flew open in surprise when the tip of his cock popped through the constricting ring of muscle and slid into her throat.

Paul cried out, his voice oddly high-pitched. His groin moved, once and then again, and he came. The first spurt of creamy fluid slid down her throat as Paul went to work on her ravaged pussy, lapping at her like a cat after cream. His tongue found and circled her hard pearl, tugging at it with his lips. He pulled her clit into his mouth, sucked, and she blew apart. Her head flying backwards, she gulped air and wailed, the force of her orgasm overpowering in its intensity. Starbursts popped behind her closed eyelids, each contraction of her walls around Will's iron cock prompting a new splash of color.

Will's fingers dug into her skin, his grip tightening almost to the point of pain, as he pumped harder and faster. He showed no mercy as he pillaged the tender depths of her channel with his thick cock.

With a ferocious growl, Will shoved unmercifully into her one last time. He came, his whole body locking up. Bone deep spasms vibrated through him and into Emma, as he filled her with his passionate release.

Will's grip loosened. His sweaty forehead rested on her shoulder. His lips ran over her feverish skin, prompting a fresh rush of goose bumps. Emma panted, attempting to regain her composure.

Paul rolled away, landing in a satiated heap on his back beside her. His legs gaped open, giving her a full view of all his goods. Emma reached out and rubbed her hand over his lean thigh, giving comfort even as she gained it.

Will stayed plastered against her back. His chest heaved under the exertion of each ragged inhalation as he too tried to regain his breath. One calloused fingertip idly drew circles over her thigh, while the arm underneath her held her tight.

Emma was content not to move at all. She wasn't even sure she could. Her body was exhausted. Taking on both men had worn her out, but it was a good, satiated exhaustion. One she wouldn't mind waking up to every day.

* * *

Paul lay still as long as he was able. When his back started to cramp, he knew it was time to move. He could only take so much inactivity before his age started creeping in on him. Oh, he knew he was still young, barely into his thirties, but sometimes his body felt older than his thirty-one years.

Swinging himself around, he flopped back beside Emma, a smile on his face. Waking up beside her this morning had been a surprise, a pleasant one, but not an expected occurrence. Will must've groveled quite a bit to get her to come home with him.

Though he'd hoped things would go well, Paul hadn't been so sure Emma would let Will into her home, much less agree to anything more after the way he'd behaved. He wouldn't have blamed her if she'd sent him packing with a knee to the balls after some of the things he'd done.

Not that Paul couldn't see both sides of the coin; he knew that Emma didn't understand why Will was being so reluctant about pursuing a relationship with her. She didn't know the kind of idiocy the two of them had been forced to endure over the years because of bigots who couldn't see that two people's love for each other could transcend sexual orientation.

He imagined a lot of the same backwoods hillbillies that spread offensive rumors about them were probably the same sickos who dressed up in sheets and paraded around demanding white power. Since they were clearly touched in the head, he tried not to let it bother him.

Will shared his sentiment, but when it came to Emma, he was like a papa Bear with a briar in his paw. The thought of opening her up to the small minds around them, seeing her hurt and likely ostracized because of who she chose to love, was more than he could stomach. There were other issues, but Paul felt sure that his inane urge to cloister Emma in bubble wrap and protect her from the world was the biggest one he was going to have to overcome.

Emma wasn't the kind of person who would stand back and let the rest of the world fight her battles for her. She may have all the classic signs of being the girl next door, but beneath her marshmallow soft facade, she possessed a core of steel. The way she'd come through Mark's desertion with her head held high and her pride intact said as much. Paul really wished he'd been around to see the reception Mark got upon his arrival home. From what he'd heard, Emma had busted out all the windows in his vintage Mustang, and sliced all four tires. The way he looked at it, the slimy little weasel had deserved that and a whole lot more.

Paul tried to be nice whenever Mark visited, but the truth was, he simply didn't like the little bastard. Other than their similar builds and physical characteristics, Mark was nothing at all like Will. He was shallow, selfish, and only seemed to be concerned with the latest vehicle he was restoring for the company he'd recently started up, or the newest airhead on his arm.

Of course, there was a silver lining to Mark's being a dickhead. It meant he and Will were able to pursue a relationship with Emma. If Mark hadn't left her at the altar, she'd be Will's sister-in-law. And how much fun would that be?

Paul's grin spread wider. He rolled onto his side, Emma's face inches from his own, and pressed a long, closed-mouth kiss to her lips. One taste of her sweet body and he was addicted, already wanting more of her.

She kept her eyes open for a minute, regarding him curiously, before settling into it and letting her eyelids drift shut. He pulled back when he felt her become comfortable. Not because he wasn't enjoying it, but because he was. Too much of her sweet lips, and he would be hard again. Tempting thought, but he didn't want to press his luck.

Paul flopped onto his back, lacing his fingers behind his head. He figured he was lucky enough that she hadn't kicked him in the head for waking her up with a little oral sex. But hell, he was only human, and those sweet whimpers she made in her sleep drove him to distraction. When she started touching herself and rubbing up against the sheets, his dick threatened a mutiny if he didn't do something to help out the poor woman.

The bed shifted as Will got up and excused himself to the bathroom. He pressed a quick kiss to Emma's temple, and reached across her to run a tender hand down Paul's arm.

Emma snuggled into Paul's heat as he watched Will walk across the room to the bathroom. His eyes followed the sway of Will's taut backside, watching the firm, pale globes of his sexy ass swish back and forth until the door closed behind him.

As soon as Paul heard the shower start, he rolled over onto his side and slung an arm over Emma. "So," he said with a wry grin. "I take it things went well last night?"

Emma laughed. "Gee, how could you tell?"

Paul shot her his best come-hither look and lowered his hand to her bottom, giving it a squeeze. "That's right, I forgot what a little vixen you are. I bet you wake up with scads of horny, naked men all the time."

"Well," she teased back, "now that you mention it..."

It was Paul's turn to laugh. She was trying to pick back at him, but the blush staining her cheeks gave away her embarrassment. Yet another thing about her he found adorable. Here they were, lying naked in bed together, his steadily growing erection pressing into the soft mound of her stomach, and she was blushing over a few quirky words.

Paul already felt an abiding affection for Emma. Her inexperience and sweet naïveté tugged at the more primal, protective instincts inside him. He didn't think it would take much to topple him over the edge of really like straight into the endless void of love.

Unlike Will, Paul felt no qualms about bringing Emma into their relationship. It was a cruel world; better to weather it surrounded by the people you love, than be adrift all by your lonesome.

Emma burrowed her face into the curve of Paul's neck and sighed. Paul ran his fingers through her silken, sleep-tangled hair, pushing it away from her face. "I'm really glad the two of you finally talked things out. There was only so much I could do. Even someone as brilliant as me would eventually run out of schemes to get the three of us together."

"You know, we didn't really talk last night, Will and I. It was more like he barged into my apartment, and took what he wanted. Not that I didn't enjoy giving him what he sought, mind you, but we didn't really discuss any of this."

Her liquid blue eyes stared up him, the expression on her face serious. "I guess I'm just wondering what happens now. I mean, where do we go from here?"

"I don't know, Kitten. I suppose we make up the rules as we go."

"Kitten? Do I even want to know why you're calling me that?"

"You make the cutest little purring noises when you…"

Emma pinched his nipple, cutting his description off.

"Hey! That hurt," he said, grabbing her devious hands and pinning them above her head. "Say you're sorry."

She smiled up at him. "Nope."

"If you're not going to apologize, then you have to kiss my boo-boo and make it feel better."

Emma snickered. "Your boo-boo?"

"Yep," he grinned down at her. "What's it going to be, words or kisses?"

Emma licked her lips, her eyes sparkling impishly. "Kisses."

* * *

Will stepped out of the bathroom in time to see Emma collapse on top of Paul. Apparently they couldn't wait for him to get out of the shower before they started back up again.

Seeing them together, Emma's graceful body draped over the lean length of Paul's, their passion-slick skin sliding against one another, made him smile.

He reached deep within himself, searching for any sign of jealousy or unease and came up empty. All he felt was satiated and happy. And, if he was going to be honest, horny as hell.

He hated to interrupt their afterglow, but they needed to get some things straight right from the get-go. "Guys, we need to talk," he said, walking over to the bed.

Emma sighed and rolled off Paul, taking the top sheet with her. She came to rest on the opposite side of the bed on which Will sat. One arm propped beneath her head, she eyed Will warily. He couldn't really blame her for her apprehension after the ass he'd made of himself lately where she was concerned.

Paul lay sprawled out over the middle of the bed. Naked and unashamed of his body, he palmed his balls and rubbed. Will's eyes strayed to his lover's half-hard cock. As he watched, it twitched and tried to re-engorge.

Paul groaned and gave Will the evil eye, or his interpretation of one. The end result was a comical raised brow and frown that reminded Will of the expression Sherlock Holmes would make when stymied by a case. All Paul was missing was the pipe.

"No more talking. It only gets us in trouble. Fucking is better," Paul murmured grumpily.

"That's all fine and good, but we need to set a few ground rules."

"Like what?" Emma asked.

Will swallowed. He wasn't sure how either one of them would take what he had to say. Paul wasn't great at keeping secrets and Emma—he didn't have a clue about her. "For instance, right now, while things are new, I think we should be careful not to let anyone find out about our arrangement."

"Why?" Both Emma and Paul asked together.

Will raked a hand through his wet hair. "I just do. Things can be hard enough on a new relationship without all the gossip and speculation. I don't want to give all the busybodies in this town reason to stick their noses where they don't belong."

"Okay," Paul readily agreed. Will noticed that his cock was back at full mast and raring to go. That meant he wasn't coherent enough to agree to anything. He'd have to be reminded again later.

Emma studied Will's face for a moment before nodding. "All right, but I won't be able to hide this from my mom forever. She's going to notice when I'm out more, and start badgering me to tell her who I'm seeing."

"I know. I wouldn't expect you to keep this quiet forever, Em."

Paul was now pumping his dick, his hips cantering ever so slightly into his fist's down stroke. Clear tears of pre-come wept from the tip, making his knob catch the morning light and glisten.

Will's mouth started to water. He glanced up and noticed a new flush spreading over Emma's cheeks and down her chest.

Oh, what the hell, he thought while bending down to take the wet tip of Paul's penis into his mouth. They could always discuss rules later.

Chapter Eleven

Emma stood at the back of the room, watching the muscles in Will's forearms flex as he wiped down the bar. It had been a slow night, not unusual for a Wednesday, and they were closing down an hour early. No real reason for them to stay open when they hadn't had more than a handful of customers since the five o'clock dinner rush.

Silently, she observed Will as he moved, straightening up and making sure the day shift would have everything they needed. The top few buttons on his white shirt were undone, giving a small glimpse of the satiny skin of his chest and the soft, sparse dark hair that covered it. At some point, when she wasn't looking, he'd rolled the long sleeves of his dress shirt up to his elbows. She couldn't see it now, not with the waist-high bar blocking her view, but her memory supplied the image of how the black jeans he wore hugged his sexy ass, and outlined the bulge behind his fly to perfection.

Emma studied his noble features: wide-set chocolate brown eyes, thick brown eyelashes and winged brows, the full jut of his plump bottom lip. Without the square jaw line and devilishly sexy cleft in his chin, he would've been boyishly cute. As it was, she found him roguishly handsome.

She tilted her head to the side, just a wee bit, and sighed. So in love with the man, she sometimes made herself sick with her mushy thoughts. She could scarcely believe she'd been involved with Will and Paul for close to a month.

After that first night, they'd been nearly joined at the hip—or more delicate parts of their anatomy—for the rest of her vacation. It was simple to hide her comings and goings from her mom while off work. The woman worked long shifts at the hospital and if Emma chose to stay out half the night, she told her she was out with friends or some such nonsense. Her mom was actually glad to see her getting out more, and had commented on it more than a few times.

Once back on her regular schedule, Emma found it hard to carve out enough time for her men, work, and sleep. Most nights, she was lucky to get more than an hour or two nap in before she was forced to sneak out of the warm, snug grip around her and drive home to a cold and lonely bed.

More and more, she found herself wanting to share her happiness with the world. She knew why Will wanted to keep things quiet. After the backlash he'd received from his relationship with Paul, he was obviously wary of advertising any more weirdness to the locals. Not that he'd said as much, but it was the impression she'd gotten. Afraid to rock the boat, she hadn't really pushed the issue with him.

She and Paul had, of course, discussed it, and were of like minds about everyone else's opinion regarding their private lives. Anyone who wanted to turn up their nose could kiss their ass.

Emma's only real concern was how her mom would react. For the last several years, ever since Mark, her mom had pestered her to death to find a man and settle down. How would she react to Emma's settling down with not just one, but two men? Emma wasn't sure. Her mom was normally open-minded and liberal in her world views. It was only when it came to Emma that her mentality reverted into a throwback from the fifties. Something both she and Will seemed to have in common. They both wanted to wrap Emma up in cotton and smother her with protection.

When Will was dark and brooding, Paul compensated by being his usual fun-loving self. Whereas she'd loved Will for what seemed like forever, her budding love for Paul, with his quirky sense of humor and innate kindness, grew by leaps and bounds every day. Though she never would have thought it possible to love two men so completely, she did. Her feelings for each of them were different, but one didn't eclipse the other. The love was just there, as if her heart expanded to make room for them equally.

She wondered what Paul had in store for them later. Earlier, when he'd come down to visit, he'd said he had a surprise waiting for them after work. Knowing Paul, it was hard to tell what sort of outlandish idea he'd come up with, but she knew it would be sexual. One way or the other, with Paul, it always seemed to be. The man thought more about his dick than was healthy.

She'd never forget the first time she'd walked in on Paul going down on Will. It was the first week they'd started seeing each other. She'd just finished her shift and hurried up to their apartment. Anxious to see them both, she'd walked right in.

They stood right in the middle of the living room. Will was sitting on the arm of the couch, naked from the waist down, with Paul attending to his engorged penis. When they saw her, Will tugged at Paul's hair, trying to unlatch his mouth. Paul just smiled around the thick cock in his mouth and kept going, his mouth bobbing up and down over Will's fat erection.

Only this time, instead of being on the outside looking in, she was part of their little ragtag group. She surprised Will by quickly shucking off her clothes and joining in.

It was later, after they all fell into a tangled mass of limbs in bed, that Will explained his reaction. Since they'd never really discussed being intimate with each other outside the trio, he'd been worried that seeing the two of them together would make her feel left out.

She quickly soothed his conscience by admitting there would be times the three of them couldn't all be together. When that happened, no matter who the odd person out happened to be, the remaining two should feel free to experiment with each other. As long as no one strayed outside of the group, everything would be fine.

The jingling bell over the door pulled Emma from her thoughts. She watched Will follow the last customer out and flip the open sign over, the opposite side showing they were closed for the night.

It wasn't often Will came in and worked a regular shift. If not for the part-timer who'd called in sick, he most assuredly wouldn't have been working with her tonight. Will preferred to work behind the scene, more comfortable in the office doing paperwork than out on the floor mingling with the customers.

It hadn't always been that way. Once upon a time, Will enjoyed being in the spotlight. Ever since he'd started seeing Paul, and his folks refused to accept him for who he was, Will shut down the part of him that flourished amid their community.

Emma shook herself out of her musings, and wiped down the last booth in the back. She carried her stack of empty beer bottles and dirty ashtrays into the kitchen.

The overhead light was off. The bar didn't serve more than munchies after seven, so the kitchen staff had shut down and left hours earlier. Only the dim glow from the streetlights outside shone through the window and illuminated her way. Even without it, time and experience would have allowed her to travel faultlessly through the entire tavern blindfolded, if need be.

She placed the black plastic ashtrays in the sink before crossing the room to dispose of the bottles in the special bin set aside for breakables. She tilted her tray, listening as each bottle hit the bottom and pinged off the others with loud clanks and rattles.

Her peripheral vision picked up movement behind her. Before she could turn to see who it was, powerful arms wrapped around her and lifted her off her feet.

Emma gasped and inhaled sharply. With the inhalation came the familiar scent of spicy cologne and warm male musk. Will. Her heart stopped trying to jump out of her chest, but still kept a fast staccato beat as she wondered what he was up to. Considering how closed-mouthed he wanted to be about their relationship, cornering her in the bar, even after hours, was something she'd never expected him to do.

One hand around her waist, Will hitched her up a little higher. His other arm slipped under her knees and swung her up into his arms. Emma settled against him, her cheek resting against his sternum, listening to the steady thump of his heart. Her fingers toyed with the open collar of his shirt.

"Just what do you think you're doing?"

"Wait and see," he answered, his deep voice reverberating against her skin, making her blood thicken and move like molasses through her veins.

"Put me down, Will!"

"Or what?"

With long strides, he carried her out of the kitchen. She was glad he didn't simply hoist her onto the serving counter. The idea was hot, but having sex on the same surface where people's food would be prepared the next day was abhorrent.

"Or I'll kick your ass, is what."

"It might be fun if I let you try to."

Emma rolled her eyes. Yeah, like she'd even really try. His ass was too fine a specimen to take a chance on messing it up. But that didn't mean she couldn't threaten it anyway. Sometimes it was fun to play a little hard to get, even if she didn't mean it.

Instead of heading into the dining room, Will slid into the storage behind the bartender's station. Emma almost wanted to complain. So many of her recurring fantasies revolved around Will trapping her behind the long, mahogany bar and taking her hard and rough, right there where anyone could walk in and catch them. Somehow, now that they were together, the idea of being caught wasn't as sexy anymore.

Will wove around stock and cases of alcohol until they were ensconced in the middle of a maze of towering boxes. His arm under her knees lowered, and Emma found herself being slid down his body.

Her breasts brushed his muscular chest, making her nipples sting with need. Her feet hit the floor, falling on either side of one of his legs. Her groin pressed down over the hard length of his sinewy thigh. She couldn't help rocking into him, basking in the delicious feel of his coarse denim jeans rasping over the junction between her thighs through the thin cotton of her khakis. Hot, liquid desire slid down her channel and pooled at the entrance to her sex, preparing her for Will's possession.

Will inched forward, both hands on her hips to steady her. His thigh stayed between hers, abrading her inflamed sex, as he nudged her back against the wall. Emma followed his lead, too interested in where he would take her, to wonder over what he was hoping to accomplish. She felt her heartbeat thundering, echoing down through her body and making her pussy clench in time with its beat.

Her back firmly pressed against the cold wall, Will's heat enveloped her from the front. She stared up into his dark eyes and swallowed, as he used the leg dividing hers to spread her feet further apart and insinuated himself between them. Large hands walked around her hips, clutched at her ass, and hauled her up tight against him. His hips pitched forward, aligning the greedy length of his hard cock with the V between her legs.

Emma's head fell back, her eyes sliding shut. A moan slipped from her mouth as he rocked into her, pressing up and down over her swollen divide.

Will groaned. Emma opened her eyes in time to see Will's mouth descending toward hers. His warm, moist lips covered hers, his velvety tongue slipping between her teeth to glide sinuously alongside hers. She shared what little breath she had, kissing him back, rubbing her tongue over his in acceptance of whatever he had in mind. She wasn't above tearing her clothes off, and making love to him right there in the dusty, smelly stockroom. As hot as he made her, she wasn't sure she'd be able to deny him, even if they had been in the middle of a parade on Main Street.

Will's chest was heaving under the exertion of each labored breath, his tongue retracted and he stopped kissing back. His lips brushed over hers as he spoke. "You have no idea how much I've wanted to do that all evening."

"Oh yes I do," she replied, lifting onto her toes so she could crush her lips to his the way she wanted. She licked the silken inner surface of his bottom lip, tasting him. "All I have to do is look at you, remember what your sexy body looks like without the clothes, and I'm ready to strip down and beg."

Will grinned. "Beg, huh?"

"Mm hmm," she muttered with a nip to his full bottom lip.

"I like the sound of that."

"I'll just bet you do."

And then they were kissing again, their arms wrapped around each other, and their bodies moving in concert as they rubbed and petted like horny teenagers.

Her shirt was tugged out of her slacks. Will's hands glided up her back and around, cupping her breasts through the stretchy material of her underwire bra. His thumbs rasped over her nipples, strumming them as if they would issue sweet music, much like a guitar's strings. He wasn't far off, since she couldn't swallow the needy moans and hungry whimpers that followed his touch.

Emma fought with the button on his jeans, finally popping it free. She guided the zipper down far enough so she could slip her hand inside and fist the thickly flared head of his erection. Her fingers met moisture, telling her all she needed to know. That he wanted her just as badly as she did him. She swirled a finger through the wet, silken fluid, spreading it over him as fast as it appeared. Her hand grasped him tight, milking him, while she stroked the sensitive groove under the flange with her thumb.

Will tugged down the cup of her bra, releasing her breasts. One hand cupped and fondled, even as the other trailed down the quivering expanse of her stomach. His fingers slipped and slid trying to free the hook clasp on the inside of her pants. Before she could free her hand and do it for him, he cursed and yanked, ripping the delicate stitches from the material. Her pants gaping open, he rammed his hand under the fabric, parted the folds of her nether lips, and sank two fingers deep inside.

Emma's pants held his hand tight against her mound, the apple of his palm massaging her swollen sex with just enough force to make her eyes blur and her pussy contract. She felt the two fingers inside her bend, Will's fingertips rimming the walls of her pussy with every undulation of his hand. When he rubbed over the hypersensitive spot deep inside her, the one only he and Paul had ever been able to locate, Emma's hips jerked forward.

She whimpered, and pumped the thick cock in her hand faster, harder. She wanted to come, but more than that, she wanted to feel Will come. To know she had the power to reduce the man she loved to a quivering, needy lump of nerve endings with only a kiss and intimate touch. The same way he affected her.

Will pinched her nipple, putting enough pressure on the nerve-enriched bud to send liquid lightning arrowing down her spine. Her cunt rippled around his fingers, clenching down, trying to suck him in deeper, as her orgasm swept over her, crashed into her like a tsunami before pulling her under.

"Oh God," she moaned. "I love you, Will."

The instant the words were out of her mouth, she regretted them. She had already exchanged avowals of their feelings for each other, but telling Will her feelings—in the middle of an orgasm no less—wasn't such a wise idea. He would have too much room to deny her declaration as some spur of the moment thing, instead of the deep, abiding emotion it was.

Her hand stilled against his still pulsing flesh. Slowly, she opened her eyes and peered up at him beneath her lashes. His cheeks were flushed with passion. A mussed lock of hair hung down over his forehead. But his eyes...his eyes were soft and dreamy. Her heart seized, a sense of hope filling her chest.

Will bent forward and brushed his lips over hers in a whisper-soft, butterfly kiss. "Emma, I—" He froze, his head tilting to the side as he listened intently to something only he could hear.

He cursed before gently extracting Emma's hand from his pants. "Stay here. The bell over the front door went off. Whoever the hell it is apparently missed the closed sign. I'll get rid of them, and be right back." He zipped his fly, wincing as he rearranged his cock and buttoned up his pants. He pressed a quick kiss on Emma's lips and hurried from the room.

A frog sat in Emma's throat as she watched him go. She was going to kill whoever had interrupted them.

Emma waited and waited some more. After straightening her clothes and smoothing a hand over her hair, Emma's impatience got the better of her. She didn't want to hide in the storeroom, like a bad secret he had to keep from everyone.

Mind made up, she stalked toward the door.

Chapter Twelve

Will's eyes had to adjust to the change in light as he came out of the storeroom. When they did, he wished he was still blind.

Mark stood there, leaning against the bar. His short light brown hair peeked from beneath a black ball cap with the words "True Love Swallows" scrawled across the bill in red glitter. Tight faded Levis, a black T-shirt, and leather jacket completed the bad boy image his kid brother had been trying to project since before he'd hit puberty.

He was the last person Will wanted to deal with at the moment. A quickly tamped rush of guilt filtered through him. He hadn't seen hide nor hair of Mark for over eight months, and should have been happy to see him. The fact that Mark was probably there to bum more money off of him alleviated a little of his guilt.

The trouble Mark tended to bring with him—usually enough to give Will a headache that lasted long after he breezed out of town—wouldn't normally be an issue. Tonight, it took every ounce of acting ability he had within his body to force a smile and cross the room without snapping.

Emma loved him. He should still be with her, holding her tight and making love, while he let her know in no uncertain terms just how much he loved her back. Instead, he was going to have to pull out his checkbook and hope Mark left before he caused too much trouble.

"Mark," Will said as he approached his brother.

Mark nodded. "Will."

"What brings you by this time of night?"

Mark scowled. "Can't a guy come to visit his only brother without having a reason?"

"Sure. You usually don't, though."

"I'm happy to see you too, Will. It just so happens that I came to share my good news with you."

Will quirked a brow. "Oh. What's that?"

He was trying not to jump to conclusions, but God only knew what it was this time. The last time he'd had good news, it was some pyramid scheme he had invested in and expected to make millions from.

Mark laughed. "Not here, man. I have cause to celebrate. Thought we could grab a bottle of the good stuff and take it back up to your place. Unless you have to check with the little woman before you let me crash with you guys. Don't know why Paul hates me so much."

"Paul doesn't hate you." *He just doesn't like you.*

"Whatever." Mark waved his comment away. "So, what do you say? Can we filch a bottle and take this conversation upstairs?"

"Yeah…uh…I guess. Let me finish what I was doing and I'll meet you out back."

"Can't Emma finish closing up for you?"

"Huh?"

"You know, Emma, my ex? I saw her car out back when I parked. Where is she anyway?"

"She's in the back. We were catching up on inventory when you came in."

"Yeah, I'll just bet you were." Mark winked. "You know she's always had a crush on you, right? If you wanted to bang the bitch, all you'd have to do is snap, and she'd drop her drawers for you."

"Mark—"

"Yeah, yeah. Watch my mouth. You know, I *am* old enough to cuss if I want now. Besides what do you care? It's not like you're interested in a sorry ass lay like her anyway. I doubt even you—someone who hasn't gotten any pussy in years—would be desperate enough to fuck that loser. Not when you have Mr. Sensitive waiting upstairs for you to cornhole him."

"God damn it, Mark! And you wonder why no one likes your ass. Keep your filthy mouth shut, or you can sleep in your damn car tonight for all I care."

At his sides, Will's hands balled into fists. Anger, hot and heavy, flowed through his veins and begged to be channeled into one good uppercut to Mark's pointed chin.

He took a step toward Mark, before he called a halt and tried to rein in his anger. Violence wasn't the answer. The only thing it would accomplish would be to muddy the water between them more.

"All right, all right." Mark held his perfectly manicured hands up in supplication. "I'm sorry. It was a joke. Don't be so damn touchy."

Mark turned and started for the exit. Over his shoulder he said, "I'll wait for you on the landing. Don't forget to bring some decent liquor out with you."

Will watched him swagger out. He shook his head and sighed. He didn't know why he put up with Mark's shit. Just because Mark was the only member of his family still talking to him didn't mean Will had to let the little bastard walk all over him.

Ever since their parents had left Will the bar instead of dividing it between the two of them like they'd always promised, Mark thought he could hit Will up for money anytime he wanted. It only got worse once his mom and dad disowned him for being gay. By that point, Will owned the bar outright, and there wasn't much they could do to change their minds. Although over the last two years, Mark had made a point to tell him that was exactly what they wished they could do. If there had been any way legal way to rescind ownership of the bar, Will was sure they would have tried. Finding out his eldest son was in love with a man had damn near killed his old man.

He was going to be forced to set the boy straight; tonight was as good a time as any. Mark could say what he wanted about him. Will didn't really give a shit. But he wasn't about to let the little twerp run his mouth about his partners.

Will turned and headed for the storeroom. He wanted to pick back up where they'd been interrupted. He hoped she hadn't grown too frustrated waiting on him.

* * *

Everything was ready. Naked, Paul sprawled across the bed and surveyed the bedroom carefully. Candles were lit, toys were strategically placed under both pillows, lube was in abundant supply, and the new black silk sheets he'd bought were spread out over the bed.

He rolled onto his side, running his hand over the ultrasoft, delicate fabric. He abhorred chintzy satin sheets. The silk set for their large bed set him back a pretty penny, but the feel of them, the ambiance they lent to the room, made them more than worth it.

His arms propped behind his head, Paul settled back against the slick pillows. Emma and Will were due home any minute. The trail of tea candles and rubbers he'd left leading from the front door to the foot of the bed should lead them right where he wanted them.

For the past couple of weeks, he and Emma had been kicking around the idea of ganging up on Will, and seducing him into a puddle in the middle of the bed. Though they'd tried a lot of different positions and combinations, the three of them had yet to do two things; he and Will hadn't been inside Emma at the same time, and he and Emma had yet to both fuck Will at the same time.

Tonight, he wanted to try out the latter. When he'd talked to Emma earlier, he'd told her to be prepared for a surprise but hadn't let on any more than that. He sucked at keeping secrets, but somehow he'd managed to keep this one under wraps. The thought of how much fun he and Emma would have torturing Will with pleasure helped.

The front door opened. Paul heard the hinges squeak and then the screen door bang shut. *Any minute now...*

Deep, rumbling laughter met his ears. *Who the hell was that?* Paul got up and quickly donned a pair of loose gray cotton drawstring shorts and rushed into the living room.

Will stood inside the door, a scowl on his face. One step behind him stood Mark. Emma was nowhere to be seen.

Paul raised his brow in confusion. "Where's—"

Will glared at Paul and shook his head. "What's going on here, Paul?"

"Well, I guess nothing, now that you brought home Mr. Wonderful."

One by one, Paul snuffed out the dozen or so candles spread throughout the living room and picked rubbers up off the floor. He sat them on the mantle before turning back to Mark and Will.

He watched with impatience as the men came into the room and sat down. Mark took the recliner, while Will chose to sit on the end of the sofa farthest from his brother. Paul walked over and perched on the arm of the couch next to Will.

Irritated by having his night ruined, Paul couldn't refrain from being a smart ass. "So, Mark, what brings you by? Out of money and in need of *another* loan?"

Mark's eyes flared, but he didn't respond. Probably because he did need a loan, and knew Paul's money was more liquid than Will's. Most of what Will had was buried in the bar or the stocks he swore by. If Mark wanted Will to fork over more cash, chances were good Will would have to take it out of their joint account, and he wouldn't do that without talking to Paul about it first.

"No. I didn't come by to borrow money. Though, now that you mention it, I am a little short on cash at the moment. With the baby coming, a little extra dough would nice."

"The baby?" Paul and Will both asked at once.

Will sat forward. "That's the news you wanted to tell me?"

"Well, it's news, but not my good news. Candy's knocked up and claiming the kid's mine, but I'm not so sure about that, you know? The tramp spreads her legs for everyone. My good news is that I'm getting married."

"Candy? As in Candy Smith, the girl you left Emma for? I didn't even know you started seeing her again." Will shook his head, obviously confused. "Wait. Does that mean you and Candy are getting married?"

"Fuck no. Like I'd give that whore my last name. I'm marrying this hot little number I met a few months back. Tiffany Stephanopoulos. Her daddy is in the oil business. The whole damn family is loaded. I've really hit the mother load with this bitch."

Paul sighed and watched the two brothers hash things out. He truly couldn't care less who the little shit had knocked up. The only thing that surprised him was that it hadn't happened sooner. That Mark had made it to twenty-eight without a string of illegitimate kids was a miracle.

Where the hell was Emma? Paul knew she had been scheduled to close the bar without Will. He knew for a fact that she had come in for her shift. What happened between then and now?

While Will was busy arguing with Mark, Paul rose to his feet and slipped from the room. After blowing out the candles in the bedroom, he sat on the bed and reached for the phone on the nightstand. He punched in Emma's number, and listened as it went straight to a recording alerting him that the caller he was trying to reach was unavailable. Either she'd turned the phone off, or was in a dead zone.

Paul replaced the phone in its cradle. His fingers massaged his temples, trying to stave off the headache he felt brewing behind his eyes. If Emma wasn't at the bar, or at home, then where else could she be?

* * *

Emma pulled out onto the highway and hit the gas. It was late, so her compact car was the only one on the road. Darkness seemed to seep into the interior, filling her with an odd sense of rightness. The inky night matched the rising turmoil brewing deep inside her.

She drove through the small town, passing closed shops with huge, dark, cavernous windows that peered out at her inquisitively, like curious eyes. At the end of Main Street, she hooked a left and accelerated, driving passed sleepy houses nestled into the hillside on her way to nowhere in particular.

Emma had never been so embarrassed in her life. *Easy? Sorry lay? Loser?* The degrading words she'd heard Mark utter replayed over and over in her mind. As did Will's refusal to take up for her. Sure, he'd told Mark to shut his mouth, but not until after he'd made a scathing remark about Paul. Apparently, it was okay for him to bad-mouth her. It's not like she meant anything to Will. She was just the easy chick he was banging because he could.

Thank God she'd managed to sneak out the back exit without anyone seeing her. It was cowardly, but she didn't give a damn. Nothing short of a natural disaster would've forced her to face either man after what she'd heard. She would have to later, but for the moment, all she could do was run. Her mind spun, her thoughts too hectic to deal with right then.

Fresh tears burned behind her eyelids, blurring her vision of the road in front of her. Finally, they broke free and overflowed, streaming down her cheeks and wetting her throat. She swiped at her face with the back of her hand, and sniffled.

Her fingers itched to pick up her cell and call Paul. Blindly, her hand reached out for her purse, intent on finding her phone. She stopped with her fingers on the strap. She couldn't call Paul. He was more Will's than hers. She didn't want to put him in the middle. It wouldn't be fair.

Her chest tightened, and she choked on the sob struggling out of her throat. Once the first broke free, a deluge of tears followed.

She thought about pulling over, about waiting out the rain just beginning to fall while she cried her heart out. It was hard to concentrate on the road and her chaotic thoughts at the same time.

Emma immediately pushed the idea aside. She wanted to keep moving, though she wasn't sure where she was headed. She just knew she had to get away. She couldn't stick around and be made a laughing stock of again. The last time had been painful, but it was nothing compared to what she was feeling now. The burning ache in her chest built until it felt like a raging inferno was ready to pop inside her rib cage.

She should have listened to her mother. Should have found a nice boring man and settled down, instead of reaching for something she knew she couldn't have. Somehow, she'd fooled herself into thinking dreams could come true.

What a crock that was.

Dreams only came true for people who were blonde and a size two, or for people who were rich enough to buy themselves their every desire. They didn't come true for small town, average nobodies like her. She should've known better.

Rain began to pour harder from the black sky. Torrential sheets of it splattered over her windshield and muddied her vision. Unsteady hands flicked at the control switch for the wipers, turning it on at full power.

The gentle back and forth swish grated on her nerves. She reached over to flip on the radio, hoping music would soothe her as it usually did. Emma hit the autotune and waited for it to scan through the stations. Hearing a song she liked, a classic R & B tune from the seventies by Aaron Neville, she extended her hand to stop the scan.

Bright lights flared through her windshield. A sharp explosion blasted into the side of her car. Glass from the side window flew inward along with the wind and rain. Terrified, Emma screamed, her hands flying up to protect her face.

The seat belt pulled tight against her breasts and across her stomach, cutting off her wind. The air bag in the driver's side door exploded, tossing her around in her seat like a crash test dummy.

An odd sense of weightlessness washed over her, and she realized she was upside down. The car was rolling, flipping side over side, as it slid down the steep incline off the side of the road.

Nausea assailed her, making the bitter bite of stomach acid rise into her mouth. Emma squeezed her eyes shut and prayed for salvation.

The roof of the car struck something huge and immovable. Emma flew forward. The seatbelt cut off her air, but didn't stop her head from slamming into the upper curve of the steering wheel. Her sight blurred and clouded.

The last sound Emma heard as darkness rushed in on her was the earsplitting shriek of metal giving way and collapsing inward.

Chapter Thirteen

Will was out of his mind with worry. The time he'd spent listening to Mark grated at his conscience. He should have been paying attention to what Emma was doing, instead of wasting time listening to his brother.

Why hadn't he started worrying about her earlier, before he threw Mark out of the house?

Hours earlier, not long after finding out Mark planned to marry some debutante he hardly knew, instead of the woman carrying his child, Will kicked the little bastard out. He was sick of listening to his fiendish schemes of attaining grandeur, and watching him shit all over the people who cared about him. Let him fuck up his life on his own. Will wanted no more part in it.

The second the door slammed behind his good-for-nothing brother, Paul was in his face, asking about Emma. He wanted to know why she hadn't come home with him, and where she was. Paul's questions drew Will up short; he didn't know the answers. When he explained how Mark interrupted them, and when he'd gone back to tell her there'd been a change of plans because of Mark's untimely arrival, she was gone.

This sent Paul into a state of panic. He'd cursed the ground Will walked upon and told him in no uncertain terms, if he'd managed to fuck things up with Emma again, Paul would kick his foot so far up Will's ass that he'd be sucking his toes till Christmas.

He and Paul had taken turns calling Emma, on her cell and at home. After several hours with no word from her, they had both hopped in the car and drove by her place. Her car missing, they didn't stop. Hell, he'd even broken down and called her mom's cell. He hadn't been sure how he would explain wanting to talk to the woman's daughter at two o'clock in the morning, but he needn't have worried about it. There was no answer to that call either.

Now, Will paced the floor. His bare feet padded back and forth over the hardwood surface, along the foot of the bed. He still wore his work clothes but, thanks to Paul's wily machinations, his white shirt was unbuttoned clear to his navel. While the blowjob Paul had offered to relax him was a nice thought, Will couldn't sit still or stop fretting long enough to take him up on it.

His arms lifted by habit, his fingers immediately scouring through hair that already stood up in odd angles and peaks on top of his head. He'd never quite understood the phrase "so aggravated I could pull my hair out," but he was beginning to. He was hard-pressed not to yank on his own.

What had he done to set Emma off? He couldn't figure it out. One minute they were fine, fooling around in the back, and the next time he looked for her, she was gone. Had he done something to piss her off? Or maybe she'd overheard what Mark said and wasn't upset with Will at all? God, it was driving him insane.

He'd long since run out of ideas about where she could be. Since he couldn't get ahold of either mother or daughter, he hoped maybe they were off somewhere together. Probably cussing men in general for the asses they were and gossiping like women were prone to do. He doubted it, but he hoped anyway.

Concern clawed at his gut, telling him something wasn't right. Something was wrong, but he couldn't figure out what to do about it. The uselessness, the not knowing, was the worst. He didn't know what he'd done to upset Emma, and couldn't find her to fix it. Utter helplessness wasn't a feeling he was accustomed to, and it was beginning to piss him off. He was used to being in charge, being the one to take care of others. Not being able to set things right—this instant—like he should, ate away at him.

"Why don't you come to bed?"

Will looked at Paul, sitting on the bed, his hands twisting in his lap. "No. I wouldn't be able to sleep anyway. Not until I know what's going on; where she is, that she's okay."

Paul stood and walked up behind him, wrapped his arms around his waist and clung to him. "I'm sure she's fine. She's just pissed is all. Probably off somewhere stewing and planning revenge on you for whatever she thinks you did wrong." He rested his forehead on the back of Will's shoulder, his cheek soft against Will's skin. "You still can't think of anything you said or did to send her off?"

Will sighed and reached back to pull Paul's arms harder around him. "No. Mark said a bunch of shit, but I shut him up. I don't know—" He shook his head. "Shit. I just don't know."

Paul kissed the apple of his shoulder, his moist breath puffing hot over Will as he spoke. "Don't worry, Bear. I'll help you get it straightened out in the morning. I'm sure it's some sort of misunderstanding. Come to bed. Try to get some sleep. There's nothing you can do right now anyway."

Will allowed Paul to maneuver him over to the bed and undress him. Naked, he slipped between the cool, slick silk sheets he only then noticed were on the bed. He made a mental note to ask where they'd come from later when he could muster the energy to give a shit. Spooning against the warm heat of Paul's back, he tried to take comfort in his lover's presence.

He was still awake when the sun began to creep over the horizon and fill the room with hazy morning light.

* * *

Pain slashed sharp and bright through the darkness that was Emma's subconscious. She came up from sleep slowly, as if she were swimming through a lake of quicksand to reach awareness. She tried to take a deep breath, and gasped, as a sharp pain shot through her chest and pressed down into her lungs. Not wanting to experience that again, she tried drawing air in through short even breaths, and was relieved when the hot pain didn't return.

It was then she felt the rest of her body. Her mouth was dry and gritty, like she'd swallowed a handful of dirt. She licked her lips, and was met with the tart taste of copper from a gash in the middle of her bottom lip. Her face felt swollen and stung in odd places.

Her eyes opened. Bright fluorescent light stung them, and forced her to drop back down to half-mast. Through slitted lids, she took in her surroundings: the white wall to her right, and a pale green curtain partitioning off the rest of the room to her left. A funky beige cotton blanket covered her legs, barely retaining enough heat to keep her toes from freezing off. Even without her sight, the abrasive smell of antiseptic and steady beat of a heart monitor somewhere beyond the curtain would have told her where she was, but it didn't tell her why.

Recollections of what she'd been through rolled over her, plunging her back into the darkness, the pain, and most of all, the debilitating fear she'd felt as she remembered her car spinning out of control and tossing her around like a ping-pong ball.

Emma whimpered. Memories bombarded her, one after another, overtaxing her with hazy information she would rather forget. Like struggling against the hands trying to pull her through the busted driver's side window, not knowing they belonged to EMTs trying to help her. A man's deep voice boomed for her to hold still, as she was gently pulled from the tin can that used to be her car. Blinding red and blue lights lit up the night as she was carted up the hill on a stretcher. A loud siren wailing on the ride to the ER, its echo making her nauseous and keeping her awake when all she wanted to do was fade back into the realm of unconsciousness. The pain and confusion of the emergency room as she was poked and prodded, examined, and put back together with bandages and antiseptic.

Somewhere during all the pandemonium, her mom had appeared at her side, like a ray of comforting sunshine after a long winter. She held her hand as the ER doctors looked her over and helped answer any questions Emma was too out of it answer on her own.

The whole experience felt like a bad dream instead of something she'd just lived through. All except one part, that is. Out of everything, one question and answer stood out in stark contrast against the others.

The doctor wanted to run X-rays on her ribs, to make sure they weren't cracked instead of bruised like he was guessing. Before that could be done, one of the nurses had asked if there was a chance she could be pregnant. Emma said no, more out of habit than with any real thought.

On the way to X-ray, she'd made them stop, admitting there was chance—albeit a slim one—that she could be pregnant. Emma didn't think she was, her period wasn't even due for a few days, but the little voice in her head wouldn't shut up until she told them what she was thinking.

Her mom cocked an eyebrow at her confession, but thankfully remained silent as a nurse drew blood and left them to wait on the results.

When the blood work came back, the bruised ribs and assortment of cuts and bruises all over her body faded to the back of her mind and ceased to matter. She underwent the X-rays needed, courtesy of a large lead sheet they placed over her stomach to protect her, but her head wasn't in it. She hardly noticed the extra weight across her abdomen and the odd mutterings of the technician as he performed his job.

Emma was pregnant.

She'd almost asked the nurse how it could be possible. Common sense had interjected, saving her further embarrassment before she made a fool of herself by asking such a dumb question.

Her mom's shocked gasp and outburst "Who's the father?" resulted in Emma burying her face in her hands and sobbing. Each rattle from her chest had prompted a stab of pain, but the tears continued without pause.

How could she tell her mom the answer to that one? That her only daughter couldn't be certain which of the two men she'd been sleeping with had knocked her up?

The simple answer was she couldn't.

She was saved from having to answer by a registrar coming into the room, requesting someone to come up front and fill out the intake paperwork for her treatment. It was the last thing Emma remembered. She must have fallen asleep waiting on her mom to finish filling out the hundred and two forms the hospital needed before they would release her. Since there wasn't a clock in the room, Emma had no way of knowing exactly how much time had passed. It could've been fifteen minutes or an hour.

Emma stretched one arm alongside the bed and searched for the call button, pressing it when she finally found it. An intercom somewhere above her blared to life. "How may I be of assistance?"

"I...um...I was wondering if someone could let me know how much longer the paperwork will take?"

"Sure, honey. Let me check on their progress and I'll let you know," the disembodied voice replied.

"Thank you," Emma muttered, the intercom cutting her off midway.

She threw back the cover over her lap and swung her legs off the side of the bed. A rush of vertigo hit her, making her head spin and her stomach clench. Her hands gripped the side of the bed, fingers biting into the foam mattress pad, as she waited for it to pass.

Hot tears burned behind her gritty eyelids. All she wanted to do was shed the nasty gown she wore, get dressed, and go home. She didn't want to think about what being pregnant meant, or how much she ached, inside and out, from everything that had happened.

After she'd slept the better part of the day away, she could continue thinking on it. That would be soon enough to figure things out. Until then, her cold and empty bed sounded mighty appealing.

Chapter Fourteen

Sleep, like the solution for cellulite, continued to elude Emma. Nearly noon, she'd been home for close to three hours, but the oblivion she wanted refused to come.

She blew out a frustrated breath and sighed. Her mind wouldn't stop running in circles. A spotlight hovered right over the very subject she didn't want to think about. More than once, she'd caught her palm resting on her lower abdomen, almost as if she could sense the life growing inside her. Each time, she yanked her hand back, stuffing it under the pillow where it belonged.

She knew she couldn't evade the subject for long. She would have to face the situation head on and make some hard decisions soon, but she didn't want to think about anything right that moment. All she wanted was a little sleep. Was that really asking so much? A few measly hours of rest, before she had to face reality? She didn't think so, but the soft knock on her front door said otherwise.

With a huff of annoyance, she sat up in bed, dragging the comforter up around her. She knew who was at the door, and had left it unlocked for this very happenstance. "Come in," she yelled.

Sure enough, her mom bustled into the apartment, looking fresh and energetic, dressed in a crisp pantsuit with her hair shellacked back into a twist of some sort, though she couldn't have gotten any more sleep than Emma had.

In her hands, she held a clear Tupperware container filled with what looked like soup. The woman couldn't cook to save her life, but she reheated a mean can of soup. Emma's stomach growled in spite of her lack of appetite.

"I thought you might be hungry when you woke up," she chirped perkily.

The happy sound of her voice grated on Emma's last nerve. "I'm not hungry. And I haven't even been to sleep yet."

Her mother sat the bowl down on top of the microwave. "I figured as much. After all, you are my daughter."

Grumpy was an understatement for what Emma was feeling. "What's that supposed to mean?"

Undeterred, and seemingly unbothered by Emma's abrasive tone, she sauntered over to the bed and sat on the edge. She laid a warm hand over Emma's cold one. "It means I figured you would be up here overanalyzing your entire life. From the look of you," she wiped a lock of tangled hair away from Emma's face, "I'd say I was right."

Emma sighed. "Not so much analyzing as trying to ignore."

"Oh, honey." Suzanne's eyes filled with compassion. "I don't think this little surprise is going anywhere." She paused, her gaze searching Emma's face for answers. "Unless you're thinking of—"

"No!" Emma cut her off. There was no way she would abort her child. It wasn't that she had anything against abortion; it simply wasn't an option for her. "I'm having it. I'm keeping the baby."

The baby. Did saying it out loud make it real? It sure felt like it. Up until right then, the embryo clinging precariously to her womb, who'd refused to relinquish its tenacious hold on life while Emma's body was battered and pummeled in the accident, had been an "it." A vague reference to something that would change her life in ways she couldn't begin to imagine.

Everything was going to change. And it scared the shit out of her.

A sad smile twisted her mom's lips. "I know you are, honey. Do you want to talk about it?"

"No. You wouldn't understand."

"I might understand more than you think."

She studied her mom's face; the tiny, almost unperceivable crinkles at the corners of her expressive eyes, the soft light of perception behind them. It would be so easy to unburden all of her fears, spill her guts, and cry on her mom's shoulder like when she was a kid. But she wasn't a child any longer. She was a grown woman, about to become a mother herself. If there was a better time for her to get her act together and stand on her own two feet, she couldn't think of one.

"I appreciate the offer, but this is something I need to deal with on my own."

"All right, if you're sure. If you change your mind, you know you can come to me. Anytime you need to. Okay?"

Emma nodded. "I know and I appreciate it, Mom. Thank you for coming to the hospital, and well, for everything. I love you."

She was immediately surrounded by the sweet smell of perfume as she was pulled into her mom's arms. "I love you too, honey. No matter how old you are, you'll always be my baby." She heard a sniffle above her head. "Even after you have one of your own."

Emma's eyes welled with unshed tears, but she blinked them back, refusing to ruin the moment. She had a lot to think about, a lot to do, and now wasn't the time to dissolve into a blubbering mess. "Think of what a hot grandma you'll make, though."

Thick, watery laughter rumbled from the chest Emma's ear was pressed against. "Now that's a hell of a thought. Me, a grandma."

Emma wiggled out of her mom's arms and sat back, contemplating her next step. She didn't look forward to it, but she needed to talk to Will and Paul. "Mom, can I borrow your car for a bit?"

"Sure. Just make sure you have it back before six. I have to work tonight."

Emma watched as she stood and swiped a hand over her clothes, straightening out invisible creases in her pantsuit.

As she neared the door, she turned back to Emma with knowing eyes. "I almost forgot; your work called several times last night and this morning. They didn't leave a message on the machine, but the caller ID picked up the number. You may want to stop by there on your way out, and let them know you're all right. Maybe inform them you won't be able to wait tables until you're feeling better."

Emma nodded, unable to form an appropriate reply. She wondered just how much her mother already knew about her situation.

* * *

Will slid behind the wheel of Paul's car and slung the pharmacy bag onto the passenger seat. He slammed the door shut so hard the windows rattled.

He knew Paul sent him on errands because he was being so testy. Paul was anxious too, but he did a better job of hiding it than Will. Will fretted and paced. Paul tried to keep himself busy by working or surfing the Internet. It was too hard for Will to concentrate for him to even bother attempting Paul's approach.

While he was out, Will figured he might as well swing by Emma's place one more time. It couldn't hurt anything to double check and make sure she hadn't come home since the last time he'd drove by, sometime after dawn. It's not like driving by her house a few times would make him a damn stalker.

Will drove on autopilot. Lines of houses, most with small decorative, though bloomless, trees and muddy brown lawns, flew by in a blur as he wound through the back streets that led him to Emma's road.

He lifted his foot off the gas, slowing as he approached her house. The driveway was empty. Will sighed and blew out the hot air filling his chest. *No one home*. The bitter disappointment he felt shouldn't have surprised him, but it did.

Just as he pressed down on the accelerator, intending to speed on past the house, something caught the corner of his eye. Will turned his head in time to see a curtain fall back into place over the front window. Someone was home. More than likely it was Ms. Taylor, Emma's mom, but maybe she would know where Emma was, if she was okay. The thought of talking to her didn't thrill him, but desperate times called for desperate measures.

Will slammed on the brakes and guided the car into the drive, thankful for its smooth handling and easy maneuverability. He jumped from the car and quickly strode up the stone-lined walkway, before he could second guess himself.

His shaky pointer finger pressed the doorbell. He waited, his foot tapping nervously on the stoop. Determination kept him rooted to his spot, while an inner monologue in his head urged him to jump back into the car before her mom came to the door. He felt like a virgin picking up his date on prom night. Which was ridiculous, considering he was thirty-five years old, and hadn't been a virgin for almost two decades.

He pressed down the doorbell again. From inside, he heard a woman say "I'm coming, hold your horses" and wanted to kick his own ass for making himself seem so impatient. He was, mind you, but he didn't want *her* to know that.

The door opened and there Ms. Taylor stood. "May I help—" Her brows crinkled when she saw Will and then she replaced the confused look with a smile. "Oh, Will. Nice to see you."

"You too, ma'am. I was wondering if you know where Emma is. I've been trying to reach her all day. About work," he quickly added. "And I haven't been able to get in touch with her." The whole spiel lasted half a second but to him it seemed he was stumbling over his words for an eternity. Even with the chill wind blowing, sweat beaded on his upper lip.

She pursed her lips, her eyes darting around him to look out at the driveway. "Emma took my car into town to run a few errands. She should be home sometime this evening. If you'd like, I'll tell her you stopped by."

Will frowned, confused. *Why wouldn't she be driving her own car?* Before he could censor his thoughts, the question popped out.

"Oh dear." She glanced up at him with softening eyes. "I told Emma to call work. It must have slipped her mind in all the excitement."

"Ma'am, I don't understand what you're saying. What excitement?"

"Emma was in an auto accident last night. She got banged up pretty good, but was lucky enough to have come out of it relatively unscathed. She's a little sore, but no serious injuries. I told her that she should call in to work, and let you all know she wouldn't be able to wait tables until she's had some time to recuperate. Her car was totaled, so she borrowed mine."

Will felt the blood drain from his face. His gaze dropped, while his brain strove to catch up with what he was thinking.

Emma was in an accident.

It was his fault she'd been upset and out driving in the middle of the night. His fault she'd been hurt.

A throat cleared. Will glanced back at Ms. Taylor. He'd forgotten all about her.

Her eyes were slightly narrowed, and she was studying him like he was a bug on a petri dish. Standing there under her scrutiny was unnerving. He wanted to ask how she *really* was, what had happened, but he didn't. He couldn't.

"I'm sorry to hear about the accident, ma'am. Give Emma our best, and tell her not to worry about work right now. I'm sure we'll be able to find someone to cover her shifts."

Will stepped back and started to turn away.

"Will—"

Ms. Taylor's voice stopped him. He glanced back at her. "Yes?"

"Thank you for being such an understanding boss. I hope that in the next few months you'll be extra lenient with Emma at work. She may not feel up to keeping her old schedule."

Will didn't know what to say to that, so he just nodded and walked away. He was anxious to get home and see if Paul had heard anything while he'd been out. If not, they were going to go out driving and see if they could track her down themselves. It was a small town, how hard could it be to find one specific car in broad daylight?

* * *

Paul pulled a loaf of bread from the wooden bread box on the counter and set it beside the jar of chunky peanut butter he'd liberated from the fridge. He wasn't hungry, but knew he needed to eat something before his blood sugar dropped too low and made him shaky.

Diabetes could be a real bitch sometimes. Other than the doctor that prescribed his glucose pills, Will was the only person who knew about his disorder. Paul didn't want anyone else to know his weakness. It was a matter of pride. Most people thought only elderly or overweight people developed diabetes. He knew differently.

He'd developed adult onset diabetes in his mid-twenties. Unaware of the condition, he pushed the fatigue and weight loss he was experiencing to the back of his mind, chalking it up to stress at work and lack of sleep, and went ahead doing the things he always did.

A collapse while playing hoops sent him to the emergency room, where he was diagnosed and lectured to within an inch of his life for not getting treatment sooner. Now, it was a simple matter of taking better care of himself, taking his pills on schedule and checking his sugar with the small glucose meter he kept stored under the bathroom sink. Usually he had no problem keeping his blood sugar at a decent level, but being upset threw it out of whack. It was low now; however, that didn't mean it wouldn't skyrocket when he least expected it.

This was why he'd sent Will to the pharmacy to pick up a new prescription for his pills and the nasty, chalky-tasting, orange glucose tablets he liked to store in the car for emergencies.

Sometimes being forced to eat, when his body wanted anything but food, was a pain in the ass. At the moment, the last thing on his mind was fueling his stomach. Concern for Emma trumped his needs, overshadowing everything he'd done this morning. She had been on his mind before his eyes had fully opened.

Will claimed not to know what he'd done to send her off, but Paul had a pretty good guess about what had done it. After he'd made Will repeat back, word for word, what had been said between him and Mark, Paul could see where Emma would be upset. At least he thought he could. It would've been easy for her to misjudge Will's lack of fight regarding the awful things Mark had said as a show of not caring enough on his part.

Paul knew better, but Emma probably didn't have as good a grasp on the relationship between the brothers as he did. He was sure all she'd heard was Mark maligning her character, and Will's lack of response. However, that didn't excuse her running off in the middle of the night, and worrying the hell out of them. When she showed back up in town, he wasn't sure if he would kiss her breathless or give her a good talking to. Maybe fuck her raw first, and then expound on the decency of not letting the people who cared fret themselves into a tizzy with worry.

Biting into his sandwich, Paul poured himself a glass of milk, and carried it into the living room. He'd just popped the last bite of his sandwich into his mouth when he heard the front door open behind him.

He turned, looking over the back of the couch, ready to ask Will if he'd thought to drive by Emma's on his way home, and choked on a mouthful of gooey, chunky peanut butter.

Dressed in a pair of pink sweats, Emma stood in the doorway, worrying her bottom lip between her teeth. Her face was littered with cuts and bruises. The biggest, most alarming bruise sat upraised in the middle of her forehead. Dried blood crusted over the gash slashing through its center.

Paul bolted to his feet and flew across the room, taking her trembling frame in his arms. He buried his face in her hair, softly kissing the top of her head. "My God, what happened to you, Kitten?"

Paul guided Emma over to the sofa and sat down beside her, never once removing his arms from around her. He was so glad to have her there, home with him where she belonged, that he didn't want to chance letting her go.

He kissed her softly, careful of her split lip, and again asked her what had happened.

Emma buried her face in his chest, and related everything that had happened to her the night before in a choked, tear-thick voice that ripped at his insides and made him gnash his teeth. She'd been out there, all alone and scared, while he and Will had been warm and safe, ensconced in their apartment, none the wiser about the danger Emma was in.

Paul wasn't a violent person, but as he listened to Emma recount her ordeal, he found his fists clenching of their own volition. A fierce need to track down the person who'd run her off the road and beat the shit out of him for hurting the woman he loved rushed through him. He swallowed down the rage, let it simmer and wane in the pit of his stomach.

Then there was the situation that put her on that dark and slippery road to begin with. Frankly, he wasn't sure who he should be more upset with. Mark for having said the things that upset Emma in the first place, or Will for not having punched the bastard's lights out for his audacity.

"Why didn't you come to me? I know you were upset with Will, but why not call me? I would have tried to explain...I would have made things better. You have to know, Kitten, I would do anything for you. I love you."

"I was so upset; I wasn't thinking clearly. All I wanted to do was get away, go somewhere alone and think things through, you know?" Emma glanced up at him, unshed tears glittering on her long, curved, black eyelashes. "I thought about calling you, but I didn't want to get you involved. It wouldn't have been fair to put you in the middle like that, maybe make you feel like you had to choose sides."

Paul shook his head, stunned by her selflessness. Leave it to Emma to think about what was fair to him, when she was the one upset and being wronged. Her caring nature was one of the reasons he loved her as much as he did, but sometimes he wished she wasn't so thoughtful, that she could put herself first.

He hugged Emma to him, careful to treat her fragile body like the delicate treasure it was to him. "Kitten, it's not about putting one of us into the middle of the other two, or making someone choose a side during a spat. It's about keeping the lines of communication open between the three of us at all times. Even when we're angry and would just as soon poke our eyes out as look at one another. If this relationship is going to work, we're all going to have to be open and honest with each other. Otherwise, it isn't going to work."

Emma shuddered against him, hiccupping out the last of her tears. She took a deep breath, as if stealing up her courage, and blew it out. "I know. That's why I came here instead of trying to get some rest first. When Will gets here, there's something I need to tell—"

The front door flew open, crashing into the wall with a loud bang. Will stormed into the room.

"Paul! We need to find—" His deep voice died out as his eyes landed on Emma.

Chapter Fifteen

Emma's eyes widened as Will flew through the room to her side. If she'd blinked, she would have missed the way his chocolate eyes misted over, and the palpable relief etched into his features once he noticed her sitting beside Paul on the sofa.

One minute she was sitting in Paul's arms. The next, she found herself perched on Will's lap, her legs dangling off to one side, ankles resting over Paul's thighs. Will's arms were around her in a hug that threatened to cut off her oxygen and so help her, she couldn't find the resolve to tell him to loosen his tight hold on her. Who needed to breathe when being in his embrace felt so damn good, so very right?

"God, baby, I was so damn worried about you. The way you disappeared on me last night, and then finding out from your mom that you'd been in an accident. I thought I was going to go crazy." He buried his face in her hair and kissed her temple. "Don't ever worry me like that again. I don't think my heart can take it."

His heart? Emma's chest clenched and burned at the mention of his. Did his words mean what she hoped? That he returned her feelings, loved her as she did him?

She tried to open her mouth and explain why she'd left the way she had, but the words strangled in her throat, refusing to come out. She muttered a weak "I'm sorry," and then tears began to well up in her eyes again, clogging her throat even more.

"What happened, baby? Tell me what happened to you last night."

She glanced over at Paul imploringly. He scooted closer to the two of them, and filled Will in on what he'd missed. Emma wanted to kiss Paul in gratitude when he left out the parts that made her sound like an overemotional ninny. Somehow, the way he retold it, made her actions sound more dignified than she thought they deserved.

The entire time Paul relayed what she'd been through, Will rubbed circles over her back, soothing her, though his body grew more tense with every passing second. Emma kept her face down, and her eyes averted, until Paul finished his abbreviated version of what she'd went through.

Of course, Paul didn't know the half of it. Neither man knew the biggest shocker, the one she was about to drop into their laps. How would they react to the news of her pregnancy? She wasn't entirely sure, but she was about to find out.

"Will, Paul, we need to talk. There's something I need to—"

A thick finger landed over her lips, silencing her. Will tilted her face up to his. "It's okay. I understand why you were so mad at me. I promise you won't have to worry about Mark being an asshole anymore. I took care of it."

She knew she was stalling the inevitable, but curiosity made her ask. "Why?"

"After you left last night, I brought Mark home. He said he wanted to talk and had some good news. As it happens, his good news was that he was getting married. That in itself would've been great, but he's clearly marrying the poor girl for her money. If that weren't bad enough, he let it slip out that he has apparently knocked up Candy."

Emma shot a glance to Paul, confused as to how this had anything to do with her, and then turned her attention back to Will.

"I don't understand."

"I can't take any more of his shit. After the way he talked about you and Paul, and then his decision to marry some debutante instead of the woman having his child—" Will shook his head. "—it's just too much. I've gotten used to being nothing more than a piggy bank for the kid, but his lack of respect for the two of you and blatant disregard for his unborn child are too much for me to deal with. I've washed my hands of him."

Emma sat up a little straighter. "I don't get it."

"I told him if he didn't do the right thing and marry Candy, to not come back around here looking for another handout. He told me to mind my own business. That he could do whatever he damn well pleased, so I kicked his ass out."

"I'm glad to hear you stood up for me and Paul, but...God, I can't believe I'm going to say this. Isn't telling him who he should marry a little high-handed of you?"

"No."

"Maybe she has a point," Paul chimed in. "I don't want to take the little jackass's side any more than she does, but it's not really any of our business which woman has the unfortunate luck of getting saddled with him as her husband."

Will's chin shot up. "How is urging someone to do the right thing being high-handed?"

Emma smoothed a wayward lock of auburn hair out his face. "I know you were just doing what you thought best, but it seems like you're less upset about the way Mark treats others and more concerned over who he marries."

Will's chest puffed up. "So you're saying he shouldn't have to marry the woman he got in trouble?"

She couldn't believe what she was hearing. Since when did being pregnant constitute being in trouble? Had they time traveled back the damn fifties when she wasn't looking?

"*Trouble?* Don't you think Candy had a little something to do with getting pregnant? The last I heard, it took more than one person to make a baby."

Paul snickered.

Will frowned. "It's the man's responsibility to protect his partner."

If that wasn't the pot calling the kettle black...

"So they should be forced into a loveless marriage because she's having a baby?"

"Yes. Their kid shouldn't have to pay for their negligence." Will looked pointedly at her. "You of all people should know what it's like to grow up without a dad."

Emma wasn't going to go there. She didn't want to touch that subject.

"What if it was me? What if I were pregnant?" *Please, please, please, don't say something ignorant.* Emma held her breath, waiting to hear his answer.

"Simple. We'd get married."

Wrong answer. She was going to give him one more chance to redeem himself. "Why?"

"Because it would be the right thing to do!"

That was not the answer she'd been hoping for.

Emma huffed. "Why would we get married? You wouldn't even know the baby was yours. It could just as easily be Paul's."

Paul laughed, causing Emma to twist around to glare at him. "What?"

"Kitten, if you ever get pregnant, the baby will definitely be Will's."

"Why do you say that?"

Paul glanced down at his hands, nervously twisting them, and then finally looked back up at Will. The look that passed between them was secretive, and caused an arrow of nervous anxiety to shoot straight to the core of her chest.

Several tense seconds, in which she wanted to scream, passed. "Well?" she prompted.

Paul wormed in closer, putting an arm around the back of Will's shoulders and the other on her hip. "It's like this," he started, the timber of his voice low and wary. "I have type 2 diabetes."

He paused and she nodded, not knowing how else to react. She didn't understand why he hadn't told her that previously, but it wasn't the end of the world. A lot of people had diabetes and lived full, healthy lives.

"It's not a big deal," he said sheepishly, "but it can have some serious side effects. One of them is retrograde ejaculation. What that means, basically, is that the nerves responsible for opening and closing the right tubes, are fucked up. When I get off, sperm shoots into my bladder instead of through my penis like it's supposed to. It doesn't affect my sex drive," he grinned, his smile a tad lopsided, "or mean that I don't enjoy the hell out of a good climax. It just means that my soldiers aren't going to be doing any traveling outside of my own body any time soon."

Paul studied her face, his lean frame vibrating with uncertainty, while he waited for her reaction. Emma didn't know what to say; her mind whirled with what he'd told her and the implications behind it.

Instead of talking, she slid off Will's lap and pulled Paul into her arms, hugged him to her breast and rocked him like the child neither knew she carried. It was the best she could do at the moment.

She knew who her child's father was. Will. And God forgive her, but she wasn't about to tell him she was pregnant. He would insist on marrying her. This coming from a man who wasn't even comfortable letting anyone outside their ménage know they even had a relationship.

He would propose, not because he loved her, not because he couldn't imagine his life without her, but because his morals would insist upon him doing what he thought was right. She couldn't live with that. She loved him, Will and Paul, more than anything, but she wasn't about to force anyone into a marriage they didn't want.

* * *

Will heard Emma's soft snuffling, and realized she was asleep. He wasn't sure how long he'd been lost in thought while the three of them cuddled on the couch, but apparently it had been long enough for his partners to both doze off.

The trust Paul showed in Emma by revealing his condition to her, something he would never do for someone he didn't care deeply about, confirmed Will's suspicion that his partner was just as in love with her as he was. The knowledge lightened the load on Will's shoulders and made his intentions to ask Emma to marry him that much more concrete. He yearned to bind her to them, to make her theirs in a more stable, permanent way.

After hearing of her accident third hand, and realizing how little claim they really had over her, Will felt listless and out of sorts. Not being notified of her accident, of having the chance to be there for her, to hold her during the ordeal she'd went through, tore him up. He wanted to protect her, take care of her, and let her know she could always turn to him for support. He'd done a shitty job of showing her that so far, but he planned to make up it up to her. He would show her that she could count on him to be what she needed in a man. From now on, nothing would be more important to him than making sure Emma and Paul were both happy and secure in their relationship.

Emma's query into what he'd do if she were pregnant reminded him that there was a very good chance she could be. At no time during the last month had anyone thought to use protection. It wasn't an issue with him and Paul, and for some reason, getting Emma pregnant had never occurred to him. Now that she'd brought up the subject, the image of her round and heavy with his child lodged in the forefront of his mind, and wouldn't shake free. He felt like a lecher, but the thought of her carrying his baby had his cock engorging and leaking steadily against the rough fabric of his jeans, desperate to fill her and make his vision a reality.

The three of them had yet to discuss children, but Paul knew Will wanted to have them someday. He wondered if Emma wanted kids. Would she be willing to give birth to his children when there was a better than average chance they would be shunned and teased because of their parents' abnormal relationship?

That thought caused his heart to beat faster, pumping blood fast and furious through his veins in disgust. Damn the consequences; if the closed-minded people in their community had a problem with them and the special love they'd found in each other, he could always sell the bar and move elsewhere. It wasn't like he had anything holding him there besides it.

Sure, he would feel a little remorse over selling the business that had been in family for so many generations, but it wasn't like said family had anything to do with him anymore anyway. They had turned their backs on him, so why should he feel guilt over letting go of his last tie to them?

Will eased off the couch and bent to pick up Emma. She would be more comfortable in the bed. He didn't want her to wake up sore, because of the awkward position she had assumed, slouched over Paul.

Sliding his arms under her knees, Will hoisted Emma up off the couch without much effort. Paul made a disgruntled snort and stretched out along the vacated couch, throwing his arm over his eyes to block out the afternoon sunlight that filtered into the room through the blinds.

Will carried her into the bedroom, and laid her out over the bed. He began pulled the shoes from her feet and let them drop to the floor. He took his hands off her and reached for the blanket slung over the foot of the bed.

She immediately rolled into a cute little ball and buried her face in the soft mound of pillows at the head of the bed. Will stood, looking down on her for a minute, thinking about how right she looked in their bed, the long curling tendrils of her silky black hair spread out over the cream duvet.

Chill bumps popped out along her arms. Will spread the cotton throw he held out over her body to keep her warm while he went and collected Paul off the couch.

While Emma slept, he and Paul needed to have a discussion. As soon as Paul gave him the green light, he would approach Emma with his desires.

Chapter Sixteen

Will pressed a lingering kiss to Paul's sleep-slackened lips. Paul sighed, squirming around on the couch a little. He didn't kiss back, but his lips curved up ever so slightly at the corners, as if whatever he was dreaming about was stupendously pleasant. Will could just imagine what his perpetually horny lover dreamt about.

He traced Paul's lips with the callused pad of his thumb. Paul whimpered, his nose twitching under Will's teasing touch.

"Wake up, sleepyhead."

"Mph," Paul murmured.

"Wake up, baby."

Paul wiggled and swatted at Will. "'M sleepin'."

"Come on, baby. Wake up. I want to talk to you about something important."

Paul's eyelids fluttered up, his jade green irises foggy with slumber. He glanced around him, as if trying to figure out where he was. "Where's Emma?"

"She's asleep. I carried her to bed after you both nodded off on the couch." Will shrugged. "I need to talk to you before she wakes up."

Paul pulled himself up and sat facing Will. "So, what's on your mind, Bear? You look entirely too serious for it to be anything I'll want to hear."

Will leaned in and pressed his lips to Paul's, silencing him. His tongue flickered out, sweeping over Paul's bottom lip, seeking entrance inside. Paul groaned, his lips parting, and snuggled closer. He teased Will's tongue into his mouth and sucked on it. When the suction stopped, Will plunged in, his tongue moving alongside Paul's, as he explored each ridge and texture of his lover's mouth.

Chest heaving, Will pulled away when Paul's hand strayed down to his groin. As much as he wanted to indulge in a little nookie, now was not the time.

Will cupped Paul's jaw, his fingers caressing his cheek. "You worry too much."

Paul snorted and sat back. "You're one to talk."

Will smiled. "Maybe so, but what I want to discuss isn't anything for you to worry about. Good news for a change, yeah?"

"So shoot. Tell me what's on your mind."

Will exhaled. "You know I love you, right?"

"Sure," Paul said with a bit of suspicion. "I love you, too. Now out with it, before I have to hurt you."

"You wish," Will responded, laughing.

Will paused dramatically, knowing it would drive Paul crazy. He couldn't help but tease him. Paul was so cute when he was all riled up. "I want to ask Emma to marry me."

Paul was quiet. Never a good sign for a man always full of energy. Finally, he shook his head. "No."

Will's mouth unhinged. "What?"

"No. I don't want you to do that. You can't ask her to marry you."

Will's gaze dropped to his hands. He pretended to study his fingers. What was he going to do? He couldn't hurt Paul, but that didn't stop him from wanting to tell his lover to go to hell. *Shit.* He would just have to take his time and prove to Paul that his marrying Emma, his love for her, wasn't detrimental and wouldn't change the love he felt for Paul.

He looked up, ready to tell Paul it would be okay. They could wait and talk more about it later. Or he'd planned to, until he noticed the ear-to-ear grin on Paul's face.

He tackled Paul, sending him sprawling onto this back. "You asshole; you had me worried there for a minute."

Paul wrapped his arms around Will's back and hugged him. "Good. It serves you right for making me wait and wonder if you'd ever come to your damn senses."

Will pressed his face in the curve of Paul's neck and nibbled on the sweet spot under his ear. "You can really be a huge pain in my ass sometimes, you know that?"

Paul moaned, and shoved his hips up at Will. Shifting, Paul put his feet flat on the couch and leveraged himself up, rutting his groin up into Will's. Even through the multiple layers of clothing they each wore, the hard ridge of Paul's cock dug into Will's pelvis.

Grunting, Paul shoved up harder, rotating his hips, seeking the friction he desired. His hands slipped between their bodies, fingers zeroing in on the snap of Will's pants and tugging the button free.

Will pushed down, lessening the space Paul's hands had to work in, cutting him off before he could slip inside and free Will's overeager prick.

"Stop," Will muttered, his cock jerking toward the fingers breaching his zipper in spite of his words.

"Mm hmm," Paul muttered, his warm, moist lips trailing over Will's cotton-covered shoulder. At the same time, the tip of one digit slid through the moisture gathering on Will's pulsing flesh and pushed it around, wetting the bulbous flare of his cock. "Want you to be a pain in my ass."

Damn, that invite was tempting. There was nothing like the feel of Paul's tight channel compressing his cock, over and over, until he exploded. But it wasn't what he had in mind for right now. Full of regret, Will backpedaled off Paul.

Rising to his feet, Will held out his hand. "Come on. We have to go wake up sleeping beauty and share our plans with her."

Paul accepted Will's hand, scrambled to his feet, and let Will guide him into the bedroom.

On opposite sides of the bed, they crawled in beside Emma. She lay on her back, her arms flung over her head, one leg straight under the blanket, the other bent, her knee peeking from beneath. Emma portrayed the very picture of wanton relaxation.

Will wasn't sure if he wanted to wake her and continue with the seduction he had planned, or cuddle up beside her and take a nap. Then she shifted, pushing her breasts up and making the noise responsible for Paul's nicknaming her kitten, and seduction won out over cuddling.

Will lay alongside Emma's slumbering body and watched as Paul did the same. One hand propped under his head, Will let the other travel gently down her side, from her waist to hip and back up again.

Everything about her was so soft and delicate, even more so now that she was hurt. They would have to be extra gentle in the way they approached loving her into submission. He wanted to soothe away her concerns, remind her of how good things could be between them, before they proposed. He didn't want to make it easy on her to turn them down.

Living out the rest of his life without Emma wasn't an option. He needed her there, with him every step of the way, to make his life worthwhile. Knowing Paul felt the same way, that he could share the burden of love with him, eased their path and made him not so afraid to face whatever troubles the future threw their way.

Will traced Emma's collarbone with his fingertips, in awe of the satiny texture of her skin. His cock reared up inside his pants, jogging his recollection of all the textures of her body, especially the divine flowering petals of her sex, their softness, their taste. He closed his eyes and groaned, trying to cool his ardor. Slow, they had to take this slow and easy. Make it all about Emma and pleasing her. He could rub one off in the shower later, after he'd seen to her pleasure.

He looked up and met Paul's eyes. The nervous anticipation he felt must have shown on his face because Paul smiled and gave him an encouraging nod, silently urging him to begin.

Will leaned in and pressed his lips to Emma's. He pulled back almost as soon as his lips touched hers, intent on keeping the kiss chaste. "Emma," he whispered against her lips. "It's time to wake up, baby."

Remnants of Emma's dream stuck with her, blurring the line between fact and fiction. Will's deep voice resonated through her mind, trying to drag her from the blissful scene in which she was immersed. In it, she was sitting on a porch swing, in front of large white house, rocking a baby swaddled in a yellow receiving blanket. Will and Paul sat beside her, smiles on their faces and an endearing look of devotion in their eyes, as they gazed at her and the newborn.

Emma started to unravel the blanket, trying to find out the baby's sex. She wanted to know whether they'd had a boy or a girl. The harder she fought to stay in the dream, to watch it unfolding, the foggier her vision grew. Will's voice lured her farther away, ever closer to consciousness.

Against her will, Emma's heavy eyelids parted and drew up, her eyesight blurry as she took in her surroundings and the men lying beside her. Both were snuggled up to her, the heat radiating from their bodies doing more to keep her warm than the blanket covering her lower torso and legs.

Along with their warmth, each man's unique smell surrounded her. The soap they shared, the potent, underlying hint of musk and man that cologne companies would make a mint manufacturing, if they could bottle it.

Propped slightly above her, Will's fingertips traced the line of her bare arm. Paul's tousled blond head lay on the pillow beside hers, one of his muscled forearms stretched out over her stomach.

Having them both there, touching her, made her feel safe and content. In their arms, she felt all was right with the world.

She lowered her arms from where they were spread out above her head, and snuck them behind her men. "I was having the nicest dream."

Will leaned closer, brushing his firm lips over her cheek. "Oh, really? And were we in this nice dream of yours?"

"Mm hmm," Emma murmured, turning her lips into Will's kiss.

Paul leaned in and kissed the side of her neck. "Just what were we doing in this dream?"

She shook her head, remembering she hadn't yet told them about the baby. "It doesn't matter."

She would have to tell them soon, but now wasn't the time. Not when so much of their relationship was still up in the air. She hadn't even broached the subject of coming out of the closet with their relationship to their family and friends yet.

"Everything about you matters to us, Kitten," Paul murmured, pressing hot, moist kisses down her throat. Will bent down and took care of the opposite side, running his tongue around the shell of her ear, causing goose bumps to rise in his wake. He pulled the loose neck of her sweatshirt to the side and continued kissing her shoulder until the material wouldn't stretch any farther.

Emma moaned, her legs moving restlessly. She ran a hand up each of their backs and into their hair. "As much as I hate to say it, I don't think I'm up for anything more adventurous than cuddling right now, guys. You'll have to take a rain check."

Will's tongue flicked over the rapid pulse beating at the base of her neck. "Do you trust us?"

Paul nipped at her ear. Emma closed her eyes and trembled. "Yes. I trust both of you."

Fingers slipped beneath the cover and toyed with the hem of her shirt, Will's judging by the calluses, and inching it up over her ribs a millimeter at a time.

"Can you trust us enough to let us love you, worship every inch of your beautiful body, without trying to do anything in return?"

Did that mean they didn't want her to touch them? "That's not fair. I want to—"

"Uh uh," Paul interrupted. "You just said you didn't feel up to doing anything. You can't change your mind now. Let us do this for you. We want to."

How was she supposed to argue with that? Her men wanted her to lie back and enjoy herself while they pleasured her. She wasn't dumb enough to turn that down.

Emma nodded. "Okay, but I get to play later, when I'm feeling more up to it."

Both men nodded, their heads resembling the bobble head that used to sit on her car's dash. She grinned. Men weren't always easy to figure out but when it came to sex, they were a no-brainer. At least these two, anyway. There wasn't anything she could do to or with them that wouldn't turn them on.

Paul tilted her face toward him and covered her mouth with his own. Firm and moist, his lips ate at her mouth, teasing her lips to part, and sinking his tongue inside. Their tongues rasped together, wet and hot, in an unhurried rhythm that incited her desire into a slow burn of awakening passion.

Hands at her hips guided her sweatpants over her bottom and down her legs. Absently, she wondered how her legs looked. Had stubble grown in overnight, since she'd last shaved? Fingers skimmed over panty-clad pussy, and she no longer cared.

Paul sucked her bottom lip into his mouth and nipped at it. Emma moaned and her hips arched of their own accord, allowing her panties to be shimmied down and discarded with her pants.

He pulled back, relinquishing his hold on her mouth. Will took his place, easily taking over where Paul left off, seducing her with lips, teeth, and tongue.

Her shirt was lifted over her breasts, the cool air hitting her nipples and making them bead. A hot, wet mouth encircled one, laving, then suckling, while Paul's smooth fingers teased the other tight bud with gentle pinches.

Sharp, liquid desire arrowed down her channel and pooled in the gateway to her sex. Above, her clit throbbed unmercifully, engorging and hardening in anticipation of what they would do next.

Will backed off, parting with her mouth, to ease her top off over her head, leaving her naked to their hungry gazes. Somehow, with both of them still completely dressed, she felt even more open and vulnerable to them. The word submissive came to mind. The thought of being at their mercy, of allowing them to do whatever they wanted to her, only turned her on more.

Will pushed Paul's hand away and fell on her breasts, nursed at her right nipple, while Paul nipped at the left. Contrary sensations bombarded her. The smooth glide of Will's tongue; the blunt edge of Paul's teeth. Each breast received equal attention, but so very different techniques. Nip and lave, suck and pull, over and over.

Emma's neck arched back, her eyes closing under the onslaught of pleasure her body was trying to decipher. Her arms slipped under and around each man, her hands gliding up and down their backs, rubbing, soothing, and enticing them silently to continue.

Two hands, one smooth and the other rough, traveled down her ribs and over the soft rise of her stomach. Emma sucked in a breath, holding it, as they continued south over her groin and through the small patch of hair concealing her mound.

Their index fingers together, they forged into the valley between her labia, opening her, spreading her like a book. Down they went, smoothing over the opening to her vagina and back up, transferring moisture over her folds and to the small kernel ready to explode above. Her hips arched, trying to get them to touch her where she needed, where she longed for them to stroke, but they evaded her clit and pushed back down over and then into her greedy, clenching pussy.

The intimate touch on her sex withdrew, followed by both men letting go of her sore, but still needy nipples.

Emma whimpered, desperate for more of what she was receiving.

"Shh," Will whispered against her lips, pressing a quick kiss on her mouth, but pulling away before she could respond. "We're not going to leave you needing, baby." His lips quickly traveled down her throat and across her chest, blazing a trail down her stomach. "I need to taste you."

Paul's lips moved to cover hers, as Will's scorching mouth covered her nether lips. His tongue furrowed through her folds, seeking and finding the center of her apex and set to drive her insane with soft, gentle laps over her eager flesh.

Emma's hips arched up off the bed, trying to get closer to Will's marauding tongue. The blunt edge of one finger slipped into the slick depths of her channel, followed by another and then both fingers were slid inside her. Will twisted his wrist, hitting her sweet spot and lights exploded behind her eyes. A kaleidoscope of colors flared behind her eyelids as her body burst with sensation.

Emma came on a strangled cry, Paul swallowing the sound of her release as he kissed her through the tremors and the aftershocks that followed.

Will pressed one last kiss to her center, and slid up the bed to lie at her side. Both men wrapped their arms tenderly across her and held her.

As soon as the endorphin rush began to fade, she felt two very stiff erections pressing into her hips. Guilt tingled at the back of her mind. She rubbed her palms over both their groins and received a pitiful moan from Paul and a grunt from Will as he removed her hand.

"This was about you, remember? You're hurt. I don't expect you to—"

"But I want to..."

Will shuffled around and pulled open the nightstand drawer. "There's something else, something more important, that you can do for us, if you want?"

Paul helped Emma sit up. She moved to the edge of the bed and tried to peer over Will's shoulder to see what he was doing. "Anything you want, within reason. I'm not up for aerobics right now, but there are a lot of other things I could be persuaded to do."

She looked to Paul, who sat slightly behind and between her and Will, to see if he knew what Will was doing. The huge smile on his face made her suspicious. "What's going on here?"

Will stood and dropped to one knee next to the bed. "This," he said, holding up a diamond solitaire on a thin platinum band. "I love you, Emma. We both do. It would make us," he glanced at Paul, who pulled her back against him and kissed her temple, "the happiest men alive, if you would do us the honor of being our wife."

Tears welled in Emma's eyes as she saw the sincerity in Will's deep brown gaze. She looked over her shoulder at Paul. "We love you, Kitten. More than words can say." He nodded at Will. "Now say yes and put us out of our misery before Will has a heart attack waiting on your answer."

Emma laughed, happy tears streaming down her face. "Yes. Yes!"

"Thank God," Will said, rising to his feet.

Emma threw her arms around his waist and hugged him to her. Paul followed suit, mashing her in the middle of a big group hug.

When they were all hugged out, and her ribs were screaming under the pressure, they reluctantly separated. Paul sat back, a self-satisfied grin on his handsome face. "I think this calls for a stiff drink. Will, why don't you run down to the bar and grab us up a bottle of something expensive."

Will smiled in answer and turned to leave the room.

"No. Wait," Emma said. "You can't do that."

Both men looked at her, confused.

"Why not?" Paul questioned.

"There's something I need to tell you both." She took a deep breath and exhaled, while Will crossed back over to the bed and kneeled in front of her.

"What is it, Kitten? What do you need to tell us?"

She glanced from one man to the other. "I'm pregnant."

Paul's mouth dropped open. "Holy shit."

Will was silent, his face to the floor.

Nervous butterflies swarmed through Emma's stomach. "Will?"

He lifted his head, showing Emma the tears that swam in his eyes. Her heart clenched in fear. And then he smiled and she knew everything was going to be okay. Better than okay, everything was going to be perfect.

The expression on Will's face softened. His hand reached out to rub her flat belly. "You're really pregnant? We're going to have a baby?"

Emma nodded, the awe in his voice unmanning her, causing her throat to close up under the emotion she was feeling.

As she was once again pulled into a warm embrace between the two men she loved more than life, Emma's only thought was how happy she was, and how glad she was she'd faced her fears and reached out to her men, braved her insecurities and gotten so much more than she ever could have dreamed in the game of chance. Emma had her something more, and no one would ever be able to take it away from her.

Epilogue

Emma drove home from the spa, her body loose and relaxed. She'd spent the afternoon being massaged, buffed, waxed, and plucked into the best version of herself she could be.

Her mind spun with wicked scenarios of the things she hoped would happen in the night to come.

As her mother was fond of saying, Emma was up to no good. Or, well, she was up to something very good depending on how the men felt about a little—okay, a whole lot—of payback. For long months, they'd tortured her with descriptions of the all the kinky, sordid deeds they planned to carry out on her body once she gave birth and had plenty of time to recuperate from delivering the babies.

Yes, babies. If she hadn't been the one lying in bed, and suffering for twenty hours, only to be whisked off to have a caesarean section after Baby B refused to turn in the right direction, to deliver two, five-pound, fraternal twin boys, Liam and Dalton, she would hardly believe her body capable of creating two such perfect bundles of joy.

Liam took after Will, with deep red hair and dark brooding chocolate brown eyes, though he possessed her peaches and cream complexion and laid-back constitution.

Dalton, on the other hand, was a wiggling bundle of energy, with pale blond hair and her own cerulean blue eyes. Retrograde ejaculation be damned, as soon as she set eyes on the second little boy the doctor laid kicking and screaming on her chest, she'd known he belonged to Paul.

Now, eight weeks after the fact, though exhausted from round the clock feedings and diaper changes, her body thrummed for some of the loving she knew her men were dying to give her. It'd been way too long since she'd last made love to her husbands, and tonight, she had big plans for them.

That morning, she'd reluctantly dropped the boys off at her mom's, for their first overnight visit. She was surprised at the trepidation she felt leaving them, but didn't give herself time to change her mind about letting her mom babysit. She was in and out of the house in less than thirty minutes, dropping off the boys and the mass of supplies they needed to get them through the night. Fretting was ridiculous; she knew they were in good hands, and would be well taken care of by their doting grandmother.

It was amazing how fast babies could bring people closer. At first, when the three of them had broached the subject of a three-way marriage with her mother, the woman had stubbornly refused to be a part of it. In no uncertain terms, she'd warned Emma that such an unorthodox arrangement would cause her and the baby she carried to be ostracized from the community.

The lecture resulted in some of Will's insecurities and protective instincts flaring back to life. Emma and Paul had to work double-time to soothe him back into submission, while waiting for their big day to arrive.

After accepting Will and Paul's proposal, Emma began to research untraditional marriage customs. She didn't like the thought of marrying one of her men and leaving the other out. Something about doing things the traditional route felt like a smack in the face to their unconventional love.

Thanks to the Internet, she stumbled upon Neopagan Handfasting. Though a ceremony between the three of them wouldn't be recognizable in the eyes of the law, the ancient ritual seemed perfect for what she desired. They could have a ceremony to bind their lives together, and share their love with the select few people there to witness their coming together.

Emma approached the men with her idea, having already contacted a Wiccan Priestess through the yellow pages who said she would be willing to perform the sacred ceremony for the three of them.

Though Will was a little hesitant at first, because the technicality of the arrangement was still unofficial, both men agreed that Handfasting seemed like a perfect alternative to the traditional wedding ceremony.

The ritual went off without a hitch, despite the fact that her mother was not there to witness her marriage to Paul and Will.

For months, she waited, growing ever bigger, for her mom to come around to the idea of her daughter's choice in spouses. It wasn't until the day she found out she was having twins, four months into her pregnancy, that she could endure the silence no longer and drove to her mother's house. The foggy sonogram of the babies and several hours' worth of conversation and tears, allowed them to finally begin mending the broken fibers of their relationship.

Since then, seeing the three of them together and how well their lives meshed, her mother had mellowed and come to welcome the guys with open arms. The two wiggling grandbabies they'd helped give her didn't hurt either.

Emma turned off onto the bumpy gravel drive that Will was forever promising to pave and never quite managed to get to. She threw the gearshift into park, turned to grab the bag containing the props she'd bought for later off the backseat, and got out of the car.

Home sweet home, she thought, as she hurried up the walk and onto the large covered porch. Even after having lived there for almost four months, it still felt odd to call the old, refurbished, Victorian-style house they'd purchased home.

Emma jiggled her key in the lock, surprised when the knob didn't turn like it should have. Removing the key, she examined it, thinking maybe she'd tried using the wrong one. Her key ring was cluttered with old keys to various different homes. Nope, it was the right one. She stuck it back in the lock and tried again. When it wouldn't turn, she grasped the door knob and shoved, thinking maybe the door was jammed.

The front door soared inward, taking her with it. Her bags were dropped to the floor, forgotten, as her hands flew out in front of her, ready to take the brunt of her weight in the fall.

She never hit the ground. Strong hands caught Emma around the waist and hauled her up off her feet. Swiveled around fast enough to make her head spin, her breasts were pressed into the broad expanse of Will's muscular bare chest.

What was he doing home? She'd sent him and Paul on enough errands that morning to keep them both busy all day so she would have plenty of time to primp and get things ready.

"Welcome home, Kitten," Paul said from directly behind her and then a dark strip of cloth was lowered over her eyes, blinding her.

"What are y'all up to?" Emma asked, a smile in her voice. She hoped they were up to the same thing she'd been planning.

"It's a surprise," Will murmured against her forehead as he jostled her around. "You didn't think we would forget today was the six week cutoff, did you?"

"No," Emma squealed, as he heaved her up into his arms like an infant. One of the sensible low-heeled black pumps she'd paired with a comfortable but nice beige linen skirt and top, slipped off her toes and clattered to the floor. She quickly nudged off its mate. The outfit was a departure from what she normally wore, mostly jeans and T-shirts, or sweats, if she was feeling particularly beat after a long night with the twins. It had felt nice to dress up for a change, but the heels had been doing a number on the soles of her feet, and she was glad to get rid of them.

Though her body hummed with nervous anticipation of what they planned to do to her, her head fell to rest on Will's chest, over the steady thump of his heart. Will's grip under her thighs tightened, and he turned with her in his arms and began to climb the stairs. She knew they were headed up the stairs because of the bumpy up and down rhythm of her ride in his arms.

Behind them, she heard Paul's heavy footsteps on the hardwood flooring and the rustle of plastic. She couldn't be positive, but it sounded like Paul was toting the bag of goodies she'd bought upstairs with them.

She felt Will changing direction again. Her toes brushed over a cool, round metal object she thought was a door handle. *Bedroom.*

She was carried farther into the room, and then Will stopped and began to lower her to her feet. He took his nice sweet time doing it, letting her body brush enticingly against his until finally her feet hit the floor and his arms fell away.

She automatically reached up to remove the blindfold, but smooth hands gripped her arms from behind and held her immobile. "Uh uh, Kitten, the blindfold stays until we say otherwise. Now, be a good girl and do as we say."

"Or what?" she asked, wondering how far they would take their domination routine.

"Or," Will said, his voice coming from a few mere inches in front of her face. "We'll be forced to tie you down, and take what we want."

His words caused excited chill bumps to race down her back and out through her limbs. Anticipation of seeing how far she could push their boundaries skittered into the pit of her stomach and gave birth to twittering butterflies.

One by one, Will began to undo the buttons down the front of her shirt. When his fingers reached the bottom, Paul let go of her hands long enough to guide the blouse over her shoulders and down her arms.

Emma's chest heaved, her nipples pressing harder against her bra. Abrasive ecru lace that framed the half-shelf cups rasped over the sensitive tips of her breasts and made them tingle. It also let her know that her breasts were on the verge of spilling out of her bra without any assistance.

Behind her, she felt Paul working at the clasp to her skirt. The delicate slide clasp gave away and it slid over her rounded hips to pool at her feet.

"Damn," Will said.

A groan sounded in front of her, deep and needy, and she knew the bra and panty set she'd settled on had done its job. Ecru lace and silk, the top consisted of a demi-bra which barely contained her breasts when they were properly situated, the bottom a thin scrap of the same material—only crotchless and undoubtedly framing the newly denuded lips of her sex, courtesy of the Brazilian wax she'd gotten hours earlier.

"You should see the view from back here," Paul grunted in commiseration with Will's groan. His grip on her wrists returned, but loosely this time, and only one-handed. The other was too busy stroking over her side and bottom, running over the thick, flesh-toned butt plug she'd inserted to help prepare her for the night ahead, to be bothered with holding her in place.

Lack of sight was killing her. Hearing their appreciation of all the pain she'd went through at the spa wasn't enough.

She wanted to see the expression on their faces, make sure the changes in her body since having the babies didn't affect their desire for her. When the moment presented itself, namely Paul's grip on her wrists loosening, Emma broke free, yanked the blindfold from her eyes and tossed it away from her.

What met her blinking eyes was well worth any mock punishments they could have threatened. Punishments she would most likely enjoy anyway, truth be told.

Naked, Will stood tall and proud. Her gaze bypassed his broad shoulders and landed on the smattering of straight, dark hair between his firm pecs. She followed it down, over his tight abs, as it thinned into a sparse arrow beneath his navel and pointed directly at what she wanted most. Framed by a thick silver cock ring, the substantial length of his cock jutted out in front of him, the wide, flared head tinted an angry red and already glistening with moisture.

Emma licked her lips and took a step toward him. It was as far as she got, before Paul's hands gripped her forearms and turning her around to face him. She caught a brief glimpse of his naked body and then his lips crashed over her own, stealing her ability to protest at his interruption of her eye candy, as his tongue speared through her lips and glided alongside her own.

She raised her hands, anxious to explore the parts of Paul she hadn't got a chance to see, but Will chose that moment to step up behind her. The warmth from his large, hard-muscled body infused her own, as he took over the job of holding her back.

Will's erection rode the crease in her bottom, pressing into the plug she wore, shifting it inside her, making her burn for him to remove it and replace it with his hard length. Paul's cock prodded the softness of her belly. Both men felt hard as steel and ready for action. Her own sex was moist and growing wetter by the second, preparing for penetration.

Since she couldn't use her hands, she settled for using what did have at her disposal to drive the men to give her what she wanted. She wiggled and squirmed, rotating her ass back at Will only to take it away and press closer to Paul when his hips started to shift against her. She pressed her breasts into Paul's chest, rubbing her stiff nipples over the smooth, hard surface of his skin. Unfortunately, that felt as good, if not better for her than it did for him, backfiring on her.

She let herself sink deeper into Paul's kiss, relishing the taste and feel of him against her. He pulled her bottom lips into his mouth and nipped it, quickly soothing the slight sting with his tongue. Emma moaned and tried to shift closer. Will's hands on her forearms held her back.

She tore her mouth away from Paul's. A growl rumbled from the back of her throat. "Damn it, do something!"

Paul smiled and rolled onto the opposite side of the bed. Will smacked her on the bottom, urging her up and onto the bed behind Paul. He quickly followed.

On her knees in the center of the bed, Emma looked from one man to the other. She finally got the good look at Paul she'd been denied. Bare, his tan skin gleamed, and an exact replica of the silver cock ring Will wore, adorned his long, narrow cock and balls.

The slighter of the two men, he was still sex personified and also the easier of them to win over. Emma lunged, tackling Paul. He went down without a fight, laughing as she climbed astride his hips.

"Impatient tonight, aren't you, Kitten?"

Will moved behind them, straddling Paul's thighs behind her. His arms wrapped around her waist, pulling her flush against him. Emma twisted her neck, looking back over her shoulder to kiss Will.

"Neither one of you had to wait over two months for sex. You had each other while I was suffering through the last couple months of pregnancy hell. I'm the one whose had to do without for the last three months."

"Oh, poor baby," Will teased, his hands crawling up her torso to cup her breasts. "We'll just have to make it up to you."

"Damn right," she said with a smile.

Paul sat up and nuzzled her tummy, kissing the faint white stretch marks and upraised pink scar across her lower abdomen. "No time like the present." He unlatched the front snap of her bra and freed her heavy, aching breasts. Will's large palms covered them, his calloused hands rasping over her tender nipples.

"Wait," she moaned, "The bag of mine that you brought in. There's something in it, I wanted to—"

"Don't need it," Paul replied, his hand foraging under the pillow and producing a big unopened bottle of lube and a tiny package that looked suspiciously like the same thing she'd bought. When he opened the little black bag and held out his hand to her, she saw that it was. Tiny silver nipple clamps lay in his palm. They weren't quite the same as the ones she'd bought—hers were gold with tiny dangling hearts—but they would do the job.

Amused, she smiled at him. "I guess great minds think alike, huh?"

"Mm hmm. Now, what do you say we put these suckers on those gorgeous nipples of yours?"

"Lay 'em on me, big boy."

Will chuckled, his big hands tweaking her nipples, making them perk up and stand harder than they already had. Wanting to arch her back and squirm closer, she forced herself to sit still while he held her breasts up and Paul opened one of the clamps and released it over her nipple.

The soft metal bit into sensitive flesh, pinching tight, stinging, but not with enough force to hurt. It felt more like a hard, tingling suction.

Paul glanced up at her, hot desire swirling amid his pale green eyes. "Everything all right?"

"Yeah," she said a tad breathlessly, "Do the other one."

He nodded and fiddled with the other clamp, slipping it open and over her neglected nipple much quicker than the first. His mouth was quick to follow, laving her nipples one at a time through the thin metal rings as Will held them up for him.

Emma moaned, her eyes sliding closed. She buried her fingers in the hair at the base of Paul's nape and held on to him. Will clung to her back, his lips against her neck, thick-muscled arms around her, holding up her breasts like divine manna for Paul to devour.

Her hips rotated, pressing back into Will and down over Paul's tumescent flesh under her. Through the slit in the crotch of her panties, she was able to feel Paul's hard cock slide through the swollen, wet, lips of her sex, the flared ridge underneath catching on her clit with every pass.

"Oh God," she moaned, awash in sensation. "Now! I need you both inside me, right now."

"Are you sure you want to do this, take us both, I mean?" Will said, his lips against her neck.

"Yes! I need you both."

Paul let the nipple he was torturing go with a wet pop. He fell to his back, pulling Emma down with him. She went willingly, covering him with her torso, kissing him with all the pent up desire inside her.

She swiveled her hips, searching for his cock, trying to align it with her needy channel at just the right angle for penetration.

Will's hands stilled her. "Hold on, baby. Let me get you ready first."

"Hurry," she begged, throwing her hips back at him.

Will groaned, his hands fisting in the silk framing her sex. He yanked, and the thin silk bit into her skin before shredding, ripping clear down the middle and in two.

"Sorry," he muttered, casting away the scrap of fabric and not sounding the least bit penitent. "I'll buy you another pair."

He shifted, and she missed the feel of him against her. Until the warm, wet heat of his mouth settled against her bottom, licking up and down the crease between her cheeks, slithered around the plug that stretched her bottom for his possession. He speared his tongue into the gateway of her pussy and skated upward, parting the slick folds of her pussy and laving her entire sex with a single-mindedness that stole her ability to think at all. Her entire being was centered on her cunt and his manipulation of it.

A finger wormed its way inside her, only to be pursued by two of its mates. With three of Will's thick fingers rammed inside her pussy and the plug in her backside, Emma felt stretched to her limit. Her body was on fire, ready for the smooth glide and stroke of friction that she needed to reach climax.

Her channel clamped down on Will's invading digits, trying to draw him in further. "Enough," she moaned, at the limit of her patience.

Will drew back, taking his prehensile tongue with him. His fingers stayed, pulling free of her clasping sex to run up and down over her folds, massaging her clit with delicate touches that only served to inflame her more.

He tugged at the plug, twisting it inside her, and began to slowly work it out. Emma bucked, crying out at the delicious burn and friction she felt as it slid free of her body.

Left aching and empty, she was just about to beg, when she felt the blunt head of Will's thick cock against her anus.

"Ready?" Will asked.

"Yes. Do it," she moaned.

Emma took a deep breath and pushed out as he began to press in. Pressure and heat consumed her as the wide head of his cock forced down on her resistant muscles. He popped through her sphincter, into the tight channel of her bottom, and slid home in one long thrust.

"Oh God...tight," Will grunted. "You feel so damn good, baby."

Emma cried out, both the pain and pleasure of him filling her almost too much to Bear. Even so, something she needed was missing. "Paul, I need you. Now!"

Paul tensed beneath her. The rounded tip of his penis nudged her clit. It danced down through her folds, finally landing at her gateway, and prodded into her pussy by the merest millimeter.

Emma's body took over from there. Her hips rotated back and down, slowly impaling her on the full length of his rigid staff. With the thick length of Will's cock already inside her, it was an exceptionally tight fit, but she was determined. She wanted—no, *needed*—to take them both.

Inch by excruciating inch, she sank down on Paul. He was breathing heavily, his chest rising and falling under with the strain of holding still while she took what she could. Behind her, she could hear Will panting as well, his prick lodged in her to the hilt, waiting to ravage the depths of her bottom as soon as she gave the okay.

When she could move down no farther, several inches of Paul's shaft still outside her body, she glanced up at Paul, giving him an imploring look he had no problem interpreting after being together for as long as they had. He reached back, grabbed the rungs on the headboard, and heaved his hips upward, sinking the last inches of his cock into her pussy in one hard lunge.

That seemed to be the signal Will was waiting for. He pulled back, withdrawing his cock until only the flared head remained inside, and instantly plunged back in. Paul shifted his pelvis, withdrawing his shaft as Will thrust in.

And that began their rhythm, Will plunging into her ass as Paul vacated her pussy. Over and over, in and out, they tormented her, while Emma panted and moaned, held immobile between their slick, churning bodies, her hands clamped on Paul's damp shoulders.

Tension coiled in the pit of her stomach, growing ever tighter, like a spring ready to break. The wet slap of flesh, the men's ragged grunts, and the cloying scent of sex in the air around them conspired against her, sending her spiraling down the road to implosion.

Her cunt began to spasm, clenching down on the hard flesh invading her body. "Oh, shit! Don't stop!" she wailed, all her concentration on the core of her body and the feel of her men making love to her.

Paul cried out, his stroke going off rhythm, levering up hard into her at the same time Will shoved inside her. His cock expanded, pulsing wildly, and she felt the hot splash of his release.

Will moaned her name, his entire body locking up, freezing, as he pumped his climax into her, filling her with his seed.

Emma was lost, the wild convulsions of her own release upon her, spinning her through the cycle of pleasure, only to leave her shaking and gasping for breath.

She collapsed in an exhausted huddle against Paul's chest, unable to move as Will gently pulled free of her body. Paul's softening member slipped from her channel. He rolled her to her side, his arms around her, as Will fetched a washcloth and cleaned them up.

The three of them lay, in a satiated pile upon the sheets, content and happy.

 **THE END**

Amanda Young

Amanda Young is a multi-published, erotic romance author. Since she tends to write whatever strikes her whimsy, all of her novels fall into various subgenres. You never know what merry adventure her evil muse will devise next.

Basically, she writes stories about people who love indiscriminately and wholeheartedly. Her characters are never perfect; they're flawed and oftentimes troubled. Which makes it that much more satisfying when they receive the happy ending we all deserve. No matter what genre her books fall into, she can guarantee they'll end with a happily ever after. In her opinion, it's just not a romance without one.

TITLES AVAILABLE In Print from Loose Id®

A GUARDIAN'S DESIRE
Mya

CROSSING BORDERS
Z. A. Maxfield

DAUGHTERS OF TERRA:
THE TA'E'SHA CHRONICLES, BOOK ONE
Theolyn Boese

DINAH'S DARK DESIRE
Mechele Armstrong

FORGOTTEN SONG
Ally Blue

GEORGINA'S DRAGON
Willa Okati

HARD CANDY
Angela Knight, Morgan Hawke and Sheri Gilmore

HEAVEN SENT: HELL & PURGATORY
Jet Mykles

SETTLER'S MINE 1: THE RIVALS
Mechele Armstrong

STRENGTH IN NUMBERS
Rachel Bo

THE ASSIGNMENT
Evangeline Anderson

THE BLACKER THE BERRY
Lena Matthews

THE BROKEN H
J. L. Langley

THEIR ONE AND ONLY
Trista Ann Michaels

TRY A LITTLE TENDERNESS
Roslyn Hardy Holcomb

VETERANS 1: THROUGH THE FIRE
Rachel Bo and Liz Andrews

VETERANS 2: NOTHING TO LOSE
Mechele Armstrong and Bobby Michaels

WILD WISHES
Stephanie Burke, Lena Matthews, and Eve Vaughn

Publisher's Note: The print titles listed above were previously released in e-book format by Loose Id®.

Non-Fiction by *ANGELA KNIGHT*
PASSIONATE INK: A GUIDE TO WRITING EROTIC ROMANCE